THE ENVELOPE

THE ENVELOPE

JOHN DURGIN

THE ENVLOPE
Copyright © 2025 by John Durgin

Published by Live Free Or Die Press

This is a work of fiction. Names, characters, places, and incidents either are the product of the authors' imagination or are used fictitiously, and any resemblance to actual persons, living or dead, business establishments, events, or locales is entirely coincidental.

Cover Art by Christian Bentulan
Interior and Ebook Formatting by Steven Pajak
Edited by Hack & Slash Editing

Contents

To my Patreon peeps

"We're gonna make it through tonight and everything's gonna be okay."

"Nothing is ever going to be okay again."

— *THE PURGE*

"If we can't live together, we're going to die alone."

— *LOST*

PROLOGUE

Maxine Kaine looked over her shoulder for her pursuers as she ran beneath the entrance to Pembroke Park. Nightfall closed in. She had survived the hunt—for now. She'd spent the last few hours hiding out in an abandoned shed at the back of Carl Aker's farm. She couldn't believe her good fortune. In past years, most of the recipients rarely had a chance to rest for even a few minutes at a time, let alone a few hours. For a moment, she imagined making it through the night. Walking into town at sunrise. Having breakfast with Dad, like nothing happened.

But then she heard approaching footsteps and chatter coming from somewhere on the farm. She was forced to make the decision to either wait it out and hope they passed or make a run for it before they got too close. She chose the latter and was glad she had when she burst through the warped door and spotted at least four town residents heading toward the shed. One of them raised a shotgun and fired at her, the shell blasting through the dilapidated wall. A second shot whizzed by her head. She hadn't waited around to allow a third shot, instead sprinting into the woods and eventually coming out near the park entrance.

Her lungs burned, but she pushed forward into the park, scanning for any place to hide and catch her breath. She took a second to pause, listening for followers. The distant barking of a dog let her know they were still on her trail. Ahead of her were two baseball fields, a softball field, and a large soccer field, all surrounded by the smothering forest. Maybe she could make it to the hiking trails that led down to the river behind the fields.

Maxine's quads throbbed, but she forced herself to run once again, as fast as her battered, malnourished body would let her. She reached the dugout of the farthest baseball field, the one closest to the woods, and leaned against the old concrete wall to get a look at how many people were trailing her. She peered around the corner, careful not to show too much and blow her cover again. The male in front of the pack was her English teacher, Mr. Roberts. He carried an ax and a look that said he'd swing at the first thing out of place. Behind his tall, lanky figure, Maxine recognized her mail lady brandishing a large machete.

Seems fitting, she thought.

It was the mail lady who likely delivered the envelope to her—the whole reason that the entire town was after her in the first place. It was the one day of the year that an entire community dreaded checking their mail. When the thought of opening the mailbox, glaring into the dark cylindrical space, and pulling out a red envelope—*the* red envelope—was what the entire population had on their mind. And this year, Maxine was the unfortunate soul to have it addressed to her.

Everyone knew not to break the rules. Which is why

Maxine now found herself hiding behind a dugout, staring at people she'd known her entire life who were now trying to kill her. The running river drowned out most of the conversation from the approaching group. With some torrential storms over the last few weeks, the water level was extremely high, unsafe to attempt to cross. But Maxine didn't think she had a choice. She peeled herself from the concrete wall and quietly walked around the side, ready to enter the trail.

Movement from the dugout caught her attention, and she turned to see what it was. A young girl sat huddled on the bench all by her lonesome, drawing on a notepad. The little girl looked up and saw her, and for a moment they both remained frozen, locking eyes on one another. The girl's expression made it clear she was battling within, determining if it was worth letting the recipient escape. Maxine was afraid to swallow the dry air assaulting her mouth, but she did so anyway, then held up her index finger to her lips, urging the kid to be quiet. The little girl nodded and went back to her sketch pad. Maxine knew it was breaking one of the rules to intentionally aid the recipient of the envelope in any way on Mail Day, but she was relieved to see that the little girl had a big enough heart to stay quiet.

"Thank you," Maxine whispered, with tears pooling in her eyes.

Then she turned and headed toward the trail, staying low in the waning daylight in hopes the dugout would block her long enough to get into the woods. As she reached the edge of the forest, the little girl screamed from the dugout, "She's over here! Going in the woods!"

Maxine's stomach tied in knots. She turned, locking eyes with the girl. A silent plea.

The girl just stared, wide-eyed, her lips trembling. Then

she whispered the words that sealed Maxine's fate, "I'm sorry . . . We have to tell."

Maxine couldn't fault her for it; she had done the same when she was younger, giving away the location of a fleeing resident who was unfortunate enough to pull the red envelope from their mailbox. She wondered if this was karma for all those years ago. She didn't have time to feel sorry for herself, though. She needed to get as far into the woods as possible before the others reached her.

The dog barked wildly, sending ice through her veins. It was Mr. Roberts's German shepherd, Harper. She'd petted him dozens of times. Fed him treats. Now his snarls were primal, his eyes empty, his only instinct to kill.

"She's entering the woods!" Mr. Roberts yelled.

Running footsteps followed, and that was all Maxine needed to enter the trail. After a few minutes of running along the dirt path, she cut through the unkempt forest and came to the river. The rushing water slammed against the large rocks scattered across, plowing through with an intensity that would be impossible to trek.

"Please . . ."

There was nowhere to go. Darkness settled in behind the swaying branches of the trees, but instead of making her feel hidden, all it did was add to the fears consuming her. If she followed the river on land, they would find her. If she tried to get to the other side, she knew she would likely drown. It was a matter of picking the lesser of two evils, and she trusted her ability in water over escaping a swarm of determined towns-folk and a rabid dog.

Maxine closed her eyes and sighed, then jumped down the washed-out embankment into the water. As soon as she touched the river, the strength of its current wrapped around her. She plunged below the surface, slamming off protruding rocks like a pinball. The back of her head cracked on a large stone, sending a jolt of pain through her cranium. She tried to scream, only to have her mouth fill with water. Even in the freezing temperature of the river, the warmth of the blood pouring down the back of her head let her know how bad the wound really was. As her body continued to travel downstream, she desperately tried grabbing onto anything that would stop her. Eventually she would reach the dam, plummeting to a sure death if she even lived long enough to make it there.

An overhanging tree root dangled over the embankment up ahead. She prayed that her timing would allow her to grab hold of it before it was too late. She zoomed toward it, struggling to stay above the surface long enough to get a good look at it. But she was determined, and when it appeared close enough to reach for, she attempted to lunge from the sharp current, wrapping her fingers around the smooth surface of the root. Maxine dug her nails into the wood, holding on for dear life. The water continued to pull at her lower half, and she heard a small *crack* in the base of the tree root.

No, no . . .

And then her prayers were answered. The root cracked, but in doing so, it bent inward, closer to the embankment. Her body slammed into the washed-out wall, but she was ready for the impact this time. She threw herself at the edge, grabbing hold of the grooves created by the overhanging tree. With all the force she could muster, she pulled her body to a hollowed space of land, remaining beneath the overhanging bank, hidden from anyone above. One false move, one mistake, would send her plummeting back below. If she could manage to remain under cover, she thought there was a good chance the water would cause the dog to lose her scent, and the residents of Pembroke would keep moving along, wondering where she went, maybe even assuming she had drowned in the strong current.

Maxine closed her eyes and cried, allowing the emotion to come for the first time all day. She took a deep breath, smelling the earthy aroma of the soil and roots around her. The water continued crashing against anything and everything in its path, determined to keep moving.

Just like you, Maxine. You need to keep moving, she thought.

She knew it was true that the longer she remained in one spot, the better the chance of them finding her. And if they did . . . She couldn't allow herself to picture what they would do to her. All she needed to do was just make it until sunrise. She'd come so far already, but her strength was dwindling. The struggle in the water drained what little she had left, leaving her weak. The only advantage she had was nightfall, now in full effect.

The running water blocked out how close they were, but she heard enough to know her pursuers were at least in the area. Crushed branches and leaves were getting louder, and the distant voices of the obsessed mob gained clarity.

"She couldn't have gone too far, she's weak. We can't let her escape," one of the men said.

"Go get her, boy!" another yelled to the German shepherd.

Then the jingling of Harper's collar moved through the darkness before the dog finally got close enough that Maxine heard him panting just over her head. She remained completely still, trying to breathe into her shirt without making any noise.

Please, keep moving, dog.

She heard its snout low to the ground, seeking out her scent. And then the sniffing stopped. The world returned to silence behind the running water. Maxine realized the group of hunters weren't talking anymore. Their footsteps had ceased. Were they gone? Moved on to another spot?

Her body was smothered by the wet dirt and muck, but she still found herself trying to burrow deeper into it, becoming one with the land. And then some dirt fell from above, landing at the base of her feet. Maxine held her breath again, locking eyes on the open space.

The dog growled.

Before she had time to consider her next move, Harper jumped down, landing on the sloped surface, sliding toward the water. He dug his claws in, desperately grabbing hold of whatever he could to prevent himself from falling into the violent water. He lifted his head, staring right into Maxine's eyes. For a second, she felt bad for the German shepherd, but then it bared its teeth, again growling at the sight of her. The dog climbed toward her, digging one paw into the muck at a time, inching closer and closer. Maxine had nowhere to go, but she tried to back up against the dirt wall even more as jagged roots poked into her back.

A terrifying bark blasted from the dog's maw, getting close enough that Maxine now felt its spittle with each war cry coming from the beast.

"Please, Harper . . . Good dog, " she whispered. Tears streamed down her face, caking the dirt sticking to her cheeks. The plea didn't work, her voice only angered the dog even more. He was now only a foot away, yet still careful enough to take his time getting to her. And then Harper snapped his teeth together, attempting to bite her ankle and drag her out of the hole. Another few inches and he wouldn't miss again. Maxine screamed, then closed her eyes in defeat, realizing that if they didn't know her exact location before, they surely did now.

Harper lunged. His teeth pierced her shin. Hot pain exploded through her leg. A sickening *crack*. White-hot agony. Her scream ripped through the trees. Instinct took over, and she kicked at Harper. The dog yelped but didn't loosen his grip. Instead, he shook his head violently from side to side, snapping the bone completely. Again, Maxine screamed. Only this time, she didn't care if they heard or not. Flashing dots swam across her vision. She was going to lose consciousness if she didn't get the dog off her. She reared back and kicked again, sending the dog sliding backward as his daggerlike teeth came loose and slid down her skin. Maxine kicked a third time, sending Harper flying toward the water. He dropped out of sight, swallowed by the darkness beyond.

An impactful splash let her know the dog had landed in the river.

"No! Harper! We gotta save my fucking dog!" Mr. Roberts yelled.

"The girl! We need to get her first," the mail lady insisted.

Maxine attempted to move and was met with another excruciating jab down the front of her left leg. She bit down on her lip, tasting blood as her teeth dug in. She shimmied to the edge of the hole in time to see Harper flailing around in the water, moving with the current at a speed that gave him no chance to swim toward land. Desperate footsteps ran through the forest above her, following the trajectory of the dog.

"I don't give a damn about her. Someone else will find

her. I can't watch Harper drown without helping him," Mr. Roberts said.

The mail lady scoffed, but then Maxine heard more footsteps following the English teacher's voice. She waited, hoping that Harper survived. He was just doing what he was taught, and she had no intention of hurting the poor animal, but she was in survival mode.

She brought her focus back to her injured leg. It was dark, but she could still see the torn pants, the shredded meat, and fragments of bone poking through. There was no chance of getting across the river now. Staying in her hiding spot was out of the question, also, because once they got the dog, the group was sure to come back and look for her.

Maxine forced herself out of the hole and looked down. She couldn't believe she had been able to make it up the steep embankment earlier. She observed the space above, looking for a place to climb to flat land. The residents were off in the distance, well out of sight but still close enough to hear faintly. Going the opposite way was the logical choice. She pulled herself up by grabbing onto a thick root, careful not to put any weight on her broken leg. Surviving the night with this injury would be nearly impossible. Hell, surviving *without* an injury had only been done twice in the history of Mail Day. She intended to be the third. With any power she had left inside of her, she pulled herself up, holding onto the root with an ironclad grip. Her leg scraped along the jagged ground, bringing on a newfound pain that she didn't think was possible. But she fought through it. Once she reached flat land, she turned over onto her back and inhaled a lungful of fresh air.

Every inch of her body hurt. She was exhausted. Afraid. But the will to live kept her going. She grabbed a thick tree branch off the ground and got to her feet. It was a little short, but it would have to do as a makeshift crutch. It was grueling, but she moved along through the woods, eventually reaching an opening that ended at the parking lot of the town junkyard that bordered the park.

Headlights approached.

Maxine sped up and hid behind one of the large metal containers where broken-down cardboard was tossed. The car's high beams blasted across the parking lot, creating strange shadows and shapes.

Did they see me?

The driver killed the car's engine. She didn't dare look around the edge, worried the headlights would display her like a deer frozen in the middle of the road before being flattened by an oncoming vehicle.

The car door opened, then softly shut. Footsteps slapped on the asphalt, heading in her direction. Her heart slammed against her chest, knowing she wouldn't be able to get away in time.

"Maxine? Hon, is that you?"

She couldn't believe it. Had she not been leaning against the metal container, she would have collapsed at the sound.

It was her dad.

Maxine leaned her head against the metal wall and cried, unable to move. She sensed him coming around the corner before he spoke again, "Oh, hon. Are you okay?"

She didn't answer, unable to speak. Her dad walked up to her and rubbed her back.

"Let's get you in the car. I can take you somewhere safe."

"No! Dad, you can't. You know the rules. I have to do this on my own."

He sighed, continuing to rub her back.

"I'm your father. Let me help you, Max."

She didn't fight it. She didn't even have it in her to fight if she wanted to. In the most vulnerable moment of her life, all she wanted was her dad. It was as if the world knew it, and in this moment, something brought him to her. He put her arm over his shoulder and guided her to the car. He opened the passenger door and helped her inside. The seat brought a sense of comfort and relief she didn't plan to feel ever again. She had sat in this exact seat countless times in her life. The first date she ever went on, her dad drove her in this car to the movie theater in Concord.

"Watch your leg, hon," he said, then shut the passenger door and walked around to the driver's side. He scanned the junkyard and then got in the car. He was also crying.

"Dad . . . please don't cry. I'm okay, really. Just a few more hours and we can go back to normal," she said between violent sobs.

He nodded and turned to face her.

"I love you, Max. I'd do anything to protect you, you know that. Especially after we lost your mom."

They rarely talked about it. Her mother was another unfortunate soul lost on Mail Day, when Maxine was only eight years old. Ever since, her dad did whatever he needed to, whatever it took to protect her.

"I know. It's not fair, is it? We lose Mom to this, and now . . ." She couldn't continue.

She closed her eyes and wept, planting her face in her open palms. Her dad rubbed her back, attempting to comfort her. Then he removed his hand and started the car. Maxine continued to cry, so exhausted she couldn't even lift her head from her hands.

She felt cold metal press against her temple.

"Dad?"

Her breath hitched. She turned, but before she could meet his eyes—

BANG!

"I'm sorry, Maxine."

The gunshot shattered the night.

PART ONE
THE NIGHT BEFORE

ONE YEAR LATER

The clock tower rang out, echoing through Pembroke as everyone herded toward the town hall like a flock of sheep being driven to their next destination. Many of the residents traveled on foot, the small town giving them no reason to hop in their vehicle and make the short drive downtown. Others —those who lived on the outskirts of the Pembroke town line —commuted from all directions. To an outsider, it might look like a celebration. It wasn't.

It was the eve of Mail Day.

Jared Cronin sat in the back of his dad's Chevy Silverado, watching familiar faces turn unfamiliar as they passed by. His family had gone the entire ride without a single word, just the sound of the radio playing classic rock at a low volume. At fifteen years old, this was the first year Jared found himself eligible for Mail Day. Whereas in years past, he'd felt sick to his stomach having to worry about one of his parents being selected, now the stress was at an all-time high knowing it could be any one of them. It wasn't just him that felt the added stress. His parents had been extra snappy with one another all week. Now, Jared almost wished they would continue their arguing instead of saying nothing at all. This was somehow far worse.

His dad parked the truck on Main Street, finding one of the last spots in the diagonal lot located in the center of the two lanes that traveled through the heart of Pembroke. The town hall was only a few hundred feet away, and just being this close to the building sent Jared's heart rate into overdrive. Maybe if he didn't get out of the truck, he wouldn't have the risk of finding the envelope in his mailbox the next morning. Maybe if they skipped town right this second, their family would be safe. To hell with the rest of the town.

Except Jared didn't really feel that way. He had friends, including his best friend, Shawn. He had family. People he cared about, all living with the same fears and concerns. Still, it didn't stop those feelings from coming, *especially* in the days leading up to this each year.

"Okay, let's get this over with, shall we?" his dad asked.

"We have nothing to worry about," his mom said, turning to Jared.

"Don't say that. There's no way to know for sure. It's false hope, Mel," his dad snapped.

"What do you want me to say, Sam? That one of us is going to draw the short straw this year? That even if we do make it to tomorrow without incident, we always have next year to look forward to?"

I take it back. I'd rather have the silence, Jared thought.

"Can we please just get in there?" he asked, bouncing his knees back and forth in anticipation.

They got out of the truck and waited at the crosswalk as

others did the same. People greeted one another, but they were far less conversational than usual. Even after going through this annually, it still never got any easier for the residents. And the short answers and blank stares would get far worse once they knew who drew the envelope. Tension was something Pembroke dealt with every single day of the year, and the eve of Mail Day was the cherry on top of the shit cake.

Jared and his parents reached the back of the line on the sidewalk, which continued to move slowly as everyone filed into the town hall. Every year, Mayor Thompson gave a speech to remind the town of the rules that everyone must obey. And of the consequences for those who don't. Thompson was a burly man who carried enough girth to be a bouncer at a nightclub, and while he seemed nice enough, nobody dared cross his path.

After what felt like an eternity standing in line, the Cronin family entered the town hall to a murmuring crowd already seated. The predominant musty smell weighed down on the nervous families, reminding Jared of old books and forgotten corners. They found three empty seats and sat down, waiting for the meeting to start. The first thing Jared noticed, located up near the podium, was the large photo of Maxine Kaine, who died last year after almost making it through the entire night. Jared couldn't believe it was her own dad who shot her in the head to help set the town at ease. He wasn't the first family member to kill a loved one on Mail Day, and he wouldn't be the last. Jared just hoped that if it was his parents who found him, they'd be willing to risk everything and protect their only son. It was a selfish thought, one that could endanger the entire town, but he didn't care.

He scanned the crowd for familiar faces, seeing some of

his friends sitting with their parents. His best friend, Shawn Spears, sat two rows in front of him. Jared couldn't hear what his parents were saying, but the look on Shawn's face told him it couldn't be anything nice. It wasn't as if these few days were the only time during the year that Mail Day came up in conversation. Jared and Shawn spent countless hours trying to determine what led to it, why the rules had to be followed, and if there were holes in the logic that would allow them to break the curse. That's what it was—a damn curse on the town. One that had little in the way of explanations, but they had seen firsthand what happens when the rules weren't followed.

The chatter quieted, and Jared turned to see Mayor Thompson approaching the stage. The large man nodded and smiled as he made eye contact with many of the residents while he passed by. Behind him, two police officers trailed—a requirement after the attempted assassination of the mayor five years ago.

Terry Horgan, a disgruntled man who had lost his wife on the Mail Day six years prior, decided to take action into his own hands and get rid of Mayor Thompson. While he wasn't given the chance to explain himself—a bullet between the eyes made sure of that—authorities later found a letter in his home that he had written before the attempt. In it, he had insisted that Thompson was part of it all, that if Pembroke got rid of him, the curse would end. He also stated that he knew who the mayor was working with to keep the curse in place. All of this, of course, was denied by Thompson.

"Ladies and gentlemen, thank you for coming tonight. I won't waste your time—nothing I say will ease your fear—but remember this: Mail Day keeps us safe. The moment we forget that . . . the moment we break the rules . . . we all pay the price," Thompson said, scanning the crowd between sentences.

Mel Cronin squeezed her son's leg, something she probably didn't even realize she was doing. Jared looked up at her and noticed she was crying. Only a few tears, but they were there.

"As is our tradition, we start tonight by honoring last year's recipient, who selflessly did what needed to be done to protect this town. Maxine Kaine was a wonderful young woman, full of promise. She did right by us, and it just goes to show that nobody is above the rest. Her father proved that, and for doing so, he is also a hero."

The crowd clapped in approval. Jared searched the audience for Maxine's dad but didn't spot him anywhere. Was he even here? Did something happen to him? On more than one occasion, surviving family members had gone on to commit suicide after losing a loved one, typically on or around Mail Day of future years as the weight of the anniversary weighed down on them. Maxine's dad didn't just lose his daughter, he'd lost his wife a few years before that. Jared couldn't imagine what sort of heartbreak the poor man went through.

"Now, we need to cover some ground rules before we send you on your way. Yes, we do this every year, and yes, we'll continue to in future years. I'm not about to give you people a reason to forget and endanger us all. First, when the recipient pulls the envelope tomorrow morning, they *must* report to the town hall within the hour. It's okay to spend some time with your family and say your goodbyes, Lord knows it may be the last time. Given that, I suggest that tonight you pack whatever supplies you think you'll need if you're the one called upon. Once we have the name of the recipient, they will be given another hour to get a head start on the residents."

Jared's hands trembled. He clenched his fists, forcing himself to breathe. He pictured it—running, hiding like a cornered animal, waiting for the killing blow. It was something he thought about a lot, yet that's all it was until it actually happened to someone. Just a thought, right?

Was it just a thought for Maxine last year?

"Once that second hour is up, the town bell will sound off at nine. That's when the hunt begins. As Mr. Kaine showed us last year, we put the town above all else, including our families. We have to. This is not a choice, and I need you all to remember that. I'll repeat it as many times as I need to if it helps get through to each of you. This is not something that one single person can put an end to, but something we must deal with *together*. While it may seem impossible to survive the night, there are two people sitting in this crowd who have proven otherwise. At this time, I ask Wes Tremblay and Christina Hendrix to stand, and stand proud."

Jared followed the eyes of the mayor to the front row, where the two past survivors of Mail Day rose to their feet, sending the crowd into wild applause. Ms. Hendrix was an elderly woman, somewhere in her eighties. She had survived back in the Fifties—1959, to be exact—before the world's technology helped aid those seeking out the recipient. Back then, she was in her twenties, spry and athletic. Now, she was just an old lady without an ounce of happiness etched on her face. It was factually correct to say she was alive, but on the inside, she might as well have died all those years ago. Behind her eyes, Jared saw no sign of life.

Wes Tremblay, however, turned to the crowd with a big, shit-eating grin, soaking in all the attention. He was treated like a celebrity around town, and one might think he had saved a baby from a burning building the way he presented himself. Mail Day had a way of bringing out one's true personality. While most of the town dreaded the day and everything about it, some thrived on the chaos and fear.

The crowd quieted as Wes sat back down, allowing the mayor to continue.

"These two are proof that it *can* be done. So, when one of you happens to find the red envelope tomorrow morning, try to keep that in mind. And remember, it's not personal. Whether it be a friend, sibling, parent, or even a lover, it's on all of us to come together and do what must be done. When the bell strikes nine the next morning, we can go back to our normal lives once again—survivor or no survivor," Thompson said while eyeing a mother in the front hugging her child. "We have some new qualified residents this year, and we know they have higher odds of being selected. While we don't know the exact odds, we know historically that more than two-thirds of the recipients have been below the age of twenty. Which means it could be one of your own children called upon to survive the night. And just like Mr. Kaine last year, you may be the one to discover where they are. You will be forced with a decision: protect the town and everyone who lives here, or protect your loved one. I'd like to stress to you all what's happened in the past when someone put a single person above the town of Pembroke."

The crowd began to chatter again as Thompson turned to a projector screen in the center of the stage behind him. He grabbed a small remote from his pocket, then clicked on the projector. Jared braced himself, but nothing could prepare him for the images. He had seen them before—every year, the mayor forced the town to look. The early photos were the worst. Grainy, distorted faces blurred like ghosts. Time had only made their horror sharper. The first image displayed a large cornfield burned to the ground like a charcoal tundra. It wasn't just the charred husks that drooped over dead, face-first on the ground. A family—neighbors of old man Carl Akers—lay sprawled across the tar-black ground with their burned insides scattered about as crows pecked at the remains. Their bodies were mutilated, unrecognizable if not for the sign dangling from one of its chains that read *Larsen Farm*. The entire family: Gary, his wife Belinda, and their two children (ages ten and eight) reminded everyone how bad things could get.

Those images would have been enough, but Thompson wasn't done. He continued his slideshow, clicking through to display similar events from past experiences where not only more deaths occurred because of someone trying to bend the rules, but also showed local businesses that had been destroyed. Lives ruined. Those incidents set the town back years, creating emotional and financial ruin.

"Tonight, we honor recipients of the past and those of the future. We also praise *Them*. The ones who give us the chance to live in exchange for a small sacrifice. Are there any questions?"

Panicked whispers spread around the crowd, their sentences intertwining to sound like a nest of angry snakes hissing through the town hall. While people talked amongst themselves, nobody actually raised their hand to ask anything. They had been through this drill every year of their lives. Jared always wondered who *Them* referred to. Who was Thompson talking about? Nobody who had seen *Them* ever lived to tell about it. The mayor cleared his throat, silencing the crowd again.

"With that, I wish you all the best, and thank you in advance for what will be the toughest day of someone's existence."

Mayor Thompson left the podium as the residents clapped. They were free to leave, but many remained seated, either waiting for the crowd to clear or trying to get over what they had just seen on the screen. Jared tapped his mom on the shoulder to get her attention.

"Yes, hon?"

"Can I go talk with Shawn for a few minutes before we leave?"

"I think we're heading out—" she started.

"Go for it, bud. We can hang around for a few," his dad said in a firm tone, letting his wife know his decision was final.

Jared didn't wait around for his mom to give her rebuttal, taking off through the sea of people to find his best friend. He spotted Shawn and his family heading toward the exit and pushed through the crowd to catch up. With his eyes focused on Shawn, Jared wasn't paying attention and slammed into the back of an adult. He instinctively looked up and realized he had collided with Christina Hendrix. The old lady almost fell over, catching herself on one of the seats at the edge of the aisle. She turned and glared at him, but as soon as she realized it was a kid, she forced a smile. Still, nothing about her eyes said she was happy.

"I'm sorry . . . I didn't see you. Are you okay?" he asked.

"I'm fine, son. It's you that I should be asking. Are *you* okay?"

"It didn't hurt."

"That's good. But I wasn't talking about bumping into a frail old lady. I mean, are you fine up here," she said, tapping on her head with a bony finger. "Are you nervous? You're one of the newly eligible, correct?"

"Y-yes. This is my first year."

"And how are you feeling?"

"I don't know. Okay, I guess."

"Well, want a word of advice from an old woman who's lived through hell? I know what it takes to survive. Listen closely . . . "

Jared nodded, his throat tightening up so much he couldn't get a word out to respond if he wanted to.

"They always search the woods first. It's where most go to hide. If you get the envelope and you want to throw the hunters off their routine, start somewhere else. The place they'll least likely search is right in front of them," she said with a wink.

"Thanks."

Christina nodded and turned back toward the exit, shuffling along with the crowd. As if Jared needed another reason to feel uncomfortable, the way she talked with him sounded like she already knew he'd be the recipient this year. He stood, frozen in place, as he watched her walk out the door. It wasn't until his parents came up behind him that he realized he'd forgotten all about talking with his friend.

"Ready, kiddo?" his dad asked.

Jared snapped out of his trance and noticed both of his parents staring at him.

"Yeah."

As they exited the town hall, he knew nothing could be further from the truth. He wasn't ready. For any of it.

Part Two
Mail Day

Shawn pulled the envelope from his mailbox, retrieving it with trembling hands as many of the town's residents crept behind him, their eyes glowing red. Shawn ran and ran, sprinting down Main Street until he'd put enough distance between himself and the hunters. As he rounded a corner and came to Pembroke Park, Jared grasped that he himself was still trailing Shawn. When Shawn realized his best friend found him, he smiled. He asked Jared if the others were close, and to help him get away. Jared didn't think twice—it was a pact they had made with one another countless times—and helped his friend get to the woods. The sky slowly blackened as if a pouch of ink had burst, the clouds darkening until they completely blocked out the sun, imitating nightfall. The trees cracked and shifted as if something massive was plowing through the forest, coming for them. As the friends stared into the dark abyss, a towering figure—it had to be at least twenty feet tall —stood behind the veil of trees. Same as the townsfolk, the silhouette had glowing red eyes full of sinister intent. It let out a bloodcurdling roar, bringing the boys to their knees—

And then Jared awoke. Drenched in sweat.

Relief from the realization that it was just a nightmare lasted only a second. Then he remembered. Mail Day. He sighed and glanced at his bedside clock: *5:00 a.m.* His alarm was set to go off at six, but there was no chance of him falling back asleep now. He kicked off the blankets, shivering as sweat cooled on his skin. His attention shifted to the backpack leaning against his closet door, and his stomach twisted inside. The stress last night, packing the bag, having the conversation with his parents about the possibility of any of them pulling a red envelope . . . it all came crashing back to him.

It was one thing to talk about it and plan for it, it was another to wake up on the day of dreading the walk to the mailbox. Jared got out of bed and yawned, deciding it was pointless to waste his time fighting for more sleep. He left his room and approached the bathroom down the hall, trying to be quiet and not wake his parents. While the odds of Jared drawing the envelope were much higher, they still stood a chance of it being one of them. He tried not just worrying about himself in the situation but sharing concern for them as well. It couldn't be easy being a parent in Pembroke.

After he relieved himself, he took a quick shower and then went to the kitchen, smelling bacon and eggs before he rounded the corner.

"Good morning, hon," his mom said from the stove.

"Smells good. Is Dad up yet?"

"Yep, he's just double-checking to make sure our survival bags are good to go. He'll be right down."

Even though they had spent a few hours before bed going through their Mail Day checklist, his dad was always overprepared. Jared liked to think some of that rubbed off on him as well. The stairs groaned under his dad's solid frame descending.

"Morning, guys. Trouble sleeping, bud? I heard the shower start before six."

"Yeah. I had to go to the bathroom and then I couldn't fall back asleep," Jared said. He had to say what was on his mind or it would drive him crazy. "Dad . . . I know we talk about this all year, but if one of you gets the envelope, I don't know if I can do this. This is the first year I'm required to search. But I don't care—"

"*Stop*. You know we can't talk about that, Jared. Especially today of all days. We've experienced what happens when someone tries to break the rules. I don't want to hear that next part come out of your mouth."

They sat in awkward silence until Jared's mom brought breakfast to the table. She placed full plates in front of her son and her husband, then sat down in her seat and cleared her throat.

"We don't talk about this at the dinner table, boys. Let's pray, for our safety and for the safety of our loved ones."

Jared always found it odd when they did this. They weren't a religious family at all. They never attended church, read the Bible, or even discussed believing in a higher power. The only time they prayed was on Mail Day. As if God—if there even was a God—would be okay with their part-time faith. Still, Jared obliged as they all held hands, and his mother said a prayer. When she was done, Jared had lost his appetite, the nerves coming vigorously. He forced the food down, knowing it might be the last full meal he had served to him.

Stop thinking that. It could be anyone.

Yeah, well, why is this feeling buried deep inside? The feeling that when that mailbox gets opened, it's going to contain a red envelope with my name on it?

Because every kid thinks this way in year one.

After they ate, there was still a little time before they needed to check the mail, so they went through the motions of being a normal family. At least Jared's parents did. He spent the time going through his notes about Mail Day—detailed events about years past and rumors of what was truly behind it all. He and Shawn typically kept all their hidden notebooks and contraband in their secret spot. Only the two of them knew about it, and Jared made sure to grab his notebook a few days earlier so he could look for any sort of help if he was selected.

He shuffled through it, scanning every page. He lost track of how long he'd been reading when his phone's blaring ringtone startled him. Jared slammed the notebook shut and shoved it into his backpack, then ran to his nightstand to see who was calling. Shawn's name displayed on the screen, bringing back thoughts of the nightmare that woke him this morning. He snatched up the phone.

"Hey, man, how's it going?" Jared greeted.

"Just swell. Last night wasn't stressful at all, huh?"

"I wanted to talk to you at the town hall, but I got stuck chatting with Ms. Hendrix. You nervous?" Jared asked.

"My parents are losing their shit, dude. Like I'm already dead or something," Shawn said. His tone indicated he was joking, but it sounded forced.

"Let's just remember what we always say to each other—"

"Shut up. It goes without saying, you don't have to ask. What did that old bag have to say to you?" Shawn asked, changing the subject. Jared got the hint, knowing he needed to be smarter and stop bringing up things that shouldn't be discussed. They never knew when or if someone was listening.

"She just wished me luck with it being my first year eligible."

He felt terrible lying to his best friend.

Technically, it's not lying. She did say that. I just didn't tell him the rest of it.

"Yeah, well . . . you wanna share some of that luck with me? I'm about to go check the mail," Shawn said.

Jared glanced over at his clock and realized it was that time. His chest clenched. Maybe if he stayed on the line forever, he wouldn't have to check the mail. Maybe time would just . . . stop.

"Yo. You there still?" Shawn asked.

"Y-yeah. Sorry. You want me to stay on the line while you check?"

On the other end of the phone, Jared heard Shawn's front screen door slam—something that annoyed the hell out of him when he stayed over, the door always whipping shut and clipping the back of his calf on the way into the house. Shawn didn't sound nearly as nervous as Jared felt, but he wondered if it was just an act to try and sound tough in front of his best friend.

"Okay, moment of truth! Drumroll, please . . ."

"Hell no. Just open the damn mailbox, man," Jared snapped.

"Fine. You're no fun. Here goes." The sound of the mailbox door whining open came next.

Jared's heart was hammering so hard he thought an alien

was about to burst out of his chest. He closed his eyes and waited for Shawn to give him the verdict.

"Bad news . . ." Shawn said quietly.

"No . . . no way. Really?" Jared asked, no longer able to hide the panic in his voice.

"Yep. My parents got the electric bill," Shawn said, then burst out laughing.

Every emotion possible fused into a giant ball of anxiety in the pit of Jared's stomach. He was relieved that his friend didn't pull the envelope. Pissed at Shawn for trying to get him worked up, but that was how they always were with each other. What good would a best friend be if you couldn't rib one another? Jared also felt something he didn't expect. Envy. Shawn knew he was safe another year. He could go back inside and finish his breakfast with a smile on his face.

"You're an asshole, you know that? I'm going to plant a fake red envelope in your mailbox next year just to get back at you. Hey, aren't your parents going to be pissed you checked without them?"

"Nah. They're arguing again inside. This day brings out the best in marriages, right? They won't even know I checked yet. But at least when I break the good news to them, they can fight about normal stuff again."

The realization that it wasn't Shawn or anyone from Shawn's family hit Jared like a rolling boulder. That increased the chances of someone from Jared's family getting the envelope. The relief he felt a moment ago vanished. He couldn't talk anymore.

"I-I need to go. I'll call you after, okay? My parents are probably a nervous wreck waiting for me right now."

"I'll be waiting by the phone. Good luck, dude."

Jared didn't move for a few minutes. He found himself

frozen in place, not wanting to leave this moment in time. His parents stirred around in the kitchen, their conversation muffled by the walls. He wondered if they were strategizing. What would they do if it was one of them? Would they intentionally search areas they knew their family wouldn't hide? Would they hop in the car and skip town? It was one thing to go all year coming up with a plan, and another for Mail Day to arrive and implement said plan. The pressure was immense, suffocating the town like a serial killer shoving a plastic bag over their collective heads.

"Jared? Hon? Can you come here, please?" his mom yelled.

He sighed and met them in the kitchen. The first thing he noticed was how pale they both were. An outsider would likely assume they were terminally ill, and in a way, they were. Getting through today just meant looking forward to next year and going through it all over again. And now they had to worry about three of them possibly getting the envelope instead of two.

"You ready, pal?" his dad asked.

"Are we ever?" Jared said.

Somehow that response got a small chuckle from his parents. He didn't mean it to be funny, but he was glad he could make them laugh in a moment like this nonetheless. His mom embraced him, squeezing tight. Jared couldn't help but notice her sobbing, felt her body gently trembling against his. When she finally let him go, Jared wiped away a tear of his own slipping down his cheek. His dad leaned against the kitchen counter, biting his lower lip as he gripped his coffee mug like it was a life preserver.

Jared stepped onto the porch and froze. The street was alive with movement—doors creaking open, neighbors stepping out in eerie unison. No words. No hesitation. Like they'd rehearsed this moment their entire lives. His stomach twisted. It was so creepy seeing everyone gravitating to the end of their driveways like a horde of the undead. He couldn't help but pray internally, hoping he witnessed someone on his street pulling out that red rectangle that haunted generations of residents. He knew it was selfish, but he didn't care.

The Newman family across the street hugged, relief etched on their face as they shut their mailbox.

Another one crossed off the list.

Sam Cronin led the way, as he did every year on their slow journey to determine their fate. En route to open the mailbox, someone screamed down the street. Jared loathed himself for immediately hoping it was someone being chosen. He turned to check the commotion, but instead of someone dropping to their knees and crying, it was the Golden family coming together for a group hug. One of happiness and not despair.

Jared's dad cleared his throat and stopped in front of the mailbox. An object as plain and simple as could be—white with a red flag and nothing more—somehow scared Jared more than anything else in his life.

His dad opened the mailbox.

Jared held his breath. For a split second, he imagined the dark void inside swallowing his father's hand, yanking him into nothingness. Instead, his dad pulled out the mail—a flyer for a local department store.

Then he saw it. A sliver of red peeking from beneath the advertisement. His stomach dropped. The world blurred.

No, no, no. Please . . .

His mom saw it next. The sound that tore from her throat was inhuman. She collapsed to her knees, hands clutching at nothing, pleading with ghosts of Mail Days past. His dad dropped the flyer to the ground, displaying the back of the red envelope to Jared as he read the name on the front of it. His jaw quivered. He looked at his wife, and all Jared could think was, *No, not my mom. Please, don't take her.*

"J-Jared . . ."

His dad reached out, the envelope in hand. He held it toward his son with nothing but remorse behind his eyes. Jared couldn't bring himself to touch it. It couldn't be real. Shawn must have called them ahead of time to play a sick joke on him, right?

But his name was right there, in all capitals. **JARED CRONIN.**

"Son. I'm so, so sorry," his dad whispered.

His mom remained on the ground, weeping so loud that many of the remaining neighbors had shifted their attention to the Cronin family. As many times as they talked about this being a possible outcome, it never truly felt conceivable. He wondered if Maxine's family looked the same way last year. Was Maxine as unprepared for it as Jared felt?

"We have an hour before you need to get to the town hall. Let's go get you prepared. I'm sorry," his dad repeated, attempting to help his wife off the ground.

"Not my boy. We can't let them take him, Sam."

"We have no choice, Mel. But we've equipped him as best we can. If anyone can do this, it's him."

"Stop it, Sam! You know that's not true! He'll die out there—"

"*Enough!* We're all stressed, but I will not have you talking that way when we have so little time left before he has to leave."

Jared heard everything they were saying, but it was as if

their voices were distant background noises. His vision blurred and his body numbed. He tried to take a deep breath, but a set of invisible hands wrapped around his throat, squeezing it in a viselike grip. His dad gently grabbed his arm, nudging him toward the house. Jared snapped out of his panic, noticing all his neighbors watching from their driveways. Some appeared sad for him, while others were relieved. Later, he knew many of them would have neither emotion but instead, they would possess the urge to kill. As though he was nothing more than a target.

The Cronin family stepped inside. The house was the same. Their world was not.

Part Three
Time To Go

His parents masked their panic with forced confidence. Jared saw through it. He didn't care. He was the one. Just as he knew he would be, like it was destiny. Even Ms. Hendrix felt it. Why else would she have given him advice? Jared continued going through the motions of gathering his stuff, hugging his parents, and doing what he assumed most of the selected did on Mail Day, but he wasn't *really* there. Physically, yes. But mentally, he was out in the woods or creeping through alleyways between buildings. He was burrowing into crawlspaces, hiding in abandoned buildings.

Even if he survived—a long shot—he'd never look at these people the same way again. What would he do if the parent of one of his friends tried to stab him in the chest with a machete? Or worse, one of his friends came after him? The only one he trusted with his life was Shawn. Not his parents, not his teachers, not police officers who on any other day of the year would serve to protect him from evil.

He checked the time, now down to thirty minutes before he needed to head over to the town hall. Shawn would be waiting for his call, but at the moment, Jared couldn't bring himself to talk with his friend. He wasn't sure he could hear the sadness, the defeat, in his best friend's voice. As it was, Jared felt himself hanging on by a thread, and one more depressing interaction might send him over the edge.

"You wanna talk about it?" his dad asked from the doorway.

Jared turned to face him, noticing his dad's bloodshot eyes as they stared at one another.

And there it is. I can't do this; I can't pretend to be strong anymore.

Jared collapsed onto the bed and sobbed. His father sat beside him, pulling him close without a word.

"We believe in you, bud. Your mom was just stressed; she didn't mean what she said earlier."

When Jared didn't reply, his dad just let him cry. The dread was more suffocating with each passing minute. Once he felt he had cried as much as he could, Jared took a deep breath and got to his feet.

"We need to leave soon."

"Hey, bud. It's okay to let it out. You sure you're ready?"

"I have no choice. And you guys can't help me, so I have to do this myself."

"Son . . . I . . ."

He stopped talking. There was nothing else for him to say. Jared was right, and his dad knew it. He knew it wasn't fair to give his dad the cold shoulder over it, especially when he might never see him again, but he couldn't stop the anger festering inside, smothering him, overtaking the fear that was there just minutes ago. While it wasn't his parents' fault he drew the envelope, *they* were the ones who lived in this town and had a child. It was selfish. They knew one day their kid could potentially be faced with this, and they still made the choice to have a child. Who could do something like that?

Jared pushed off the bed, avoiding eye contact with his dad. He walked to his dresser and picked up the backpack, ready to face the hell that lay ahead of him.

"Please don't shut us out right now, Jared. This is awful . . . for all of us. Please—"

Jared snapped.

"'Awful for all of us'? Why the hell did you guys even have a kid? Why did you make the choice to have me, knowing I could die someday? Knowing you might be the ones to kill me. If this town wants the stupid pact to end, just stop having fucking kids!"

Cursing was not something his parents condoned under their roof, even in this circumstance. Jared immediately regretted using those words, but his dad didn't look mad. Instead, he closed his eyes and rubbed his temple with his hand.

"There are certain things that we have no control over, Jared. We . . . We're required to have kids here. To keep the cycle going. To make sure *They* get what they need from us."

Jared had gone his entire life having no idea why the town carried these dark secrets or who knew more details about them. His parents had always played it off as if they had no idea why they were forced to take part in some sick game of life or death. Everything his dad just told him contradicted that.

"What are you talking about? What do you mean, 'We're *required* to have kids'? And who are '*They*'?"

"Bud . . . you have to understand, we can't say certain

things. We don't even have the answers you want, just enough to know how dangerous it is to talk about out loud."

"More dangerous than the town trying to kill me? I think maybe I deserve to know, don't you?" Jared snapped.

His dad sighed and got up from the bed.

"Yes. We owe you that. Let's go talk with your mother before we need to head down to the town hall."

Jared stood in shock. He didn't actually expect his dad to agree. As they headed toward the kitchen, he wasn't so sure he really wanted to know.

***

With only fifteen minutes until they needed to leave for the town hall, Jared's parents turned his world upside down. They all sat at the kitchen table, waiting for someone to break the awkward silence. Jared's mom went first.

"You know anything we keep from you is only for your protection, right?" When he didn't respond, she continued. "We need you to believe that we don't have all the information. We were only told what we needed to know to keep this thing going. There are far more rules than just those that must be followed on Mail Day, Jared. Things that need to be followed every day of the year to keep this community whole, to give *Them* what they need to allow us to live normal lives."

"How's this *normal?*"

"Please, let your mother talk. We don't have much time," his dad said calmly, nodding for his wife to continue.

"I'm afraid this will just create more confusion for you, Jared, on a day when I don't want to do that to you. The thing is, we know rules that need to be followed—beyond just the main list we cover the night before—but we don't know why they're in place. Things like continuing to reproduce for new generations or not talking about it with people from out of town. You wouldn't know this because it hasn't happened since you were a baby, but we've seen the consequences. Those snapshots the mayor shares every year are just the tip of the iceberg."

"Guys . . . we need to go. I'm sorry, Jared. You know we can't be late for the town hall. If we are, the hunt begins immediately," his dad said.

Jared contemplated everything his mom had just told him, trying to wrap his head around it. He knew everyone felt trapped, he just didn't realize to what extent. He wanted to ask more, but they had to leave. His heart went into rapid-fire mode, everything finally hitting him as the shock wore off and transitioned back to fear, like a sadistic yo-yo.

He needed a plan. Many of the selected in past years died because they suffered from too much shell shock to develop a strategy. He couldn't let that be what ended his life.

Think, damn it. Where's the best place to start? Eventually I have to get to the hiding spot. Shawn won't tell anyone about it. I'll be safe there.

They loaded up the truck and rode to the town hall in silence. Jared attempted to calm himself the entire ride, failing miserably. When they pulled into the parking lot, numerous residents mingled around their vehicles, and Jared couldn't help but loathe every one of them. They were here to see the spectacle, no longer concerned about their own well-being. They knew that while Jared would try to get away, and they might get hurt during the hunt, he couldn't kill them. That wasn't how this deal worked. While everybody would say to someone's face that they never wanted to see a child selected, Jared knew full well that it made all the townsfolk happy. A child was innocent. A child was weak. Easy to find. Easy to *kill.*

He had planned, strategized, ran through every possible escape. None of it mattered. He was going to die today. Again, he cried, burying his face into his shirt to wipe away the tears. When his dad shut the truck off, his parents turned to face him in the back seat.

"Okay, this is when the mayor announces who pulled the envelope. Stay strong, and whatever you do, don't tell anyone what you're thinking of doing, son. Not even us. We can't know. And some of those people in there, they'll try to trick you. They want the immunity that comes with getting you first," his dad said.

They got out of the truck, and while the official announcement hadn't been made yet, Pembroke was a small town. Everyone in his neighborhood witnessed the scene on his front lawn this morning. His parents forced smiles as best they could, but Jared saw it behind all the residents' eyes: Every single one of them was pondering various ways to kill. To save themselves in the future. To them, Jared was now just a sacrifice.

The residents gathered in eerie silence, the town common packed shoulder to shoulder. The clock tower loomed above, casting deep shadows over the stage—as if it, too, was waiting for the sacrifice. Mayor Thompson stood on the stage with a smile on his face, seemingly enjoying every second of this. Jared felt eyes burning into him as his family forced their way through the crowd toward the front.

"Gather around everyone, we don't have much time. As is tradition on Mail Day, would this year's recipient please come forward?" Mayor Thompson yelled over the murmuring crowd.

The group parted down the middle, creating a clear path in front of Jared. They all watched him, waiting for him to go up and complete his initiation so the festivities could begin. His mom rubbed his back, but he ignored her desperate sympathy and made his way up the steps. Once he got close enough to the mayor that he could smell his cheap cologne, he turned and faced the entire crowd. From his elevated point of view, the swarm of people appeared to amplify, going as far back as he could see. All it did was confirm that there was only a tiny sliver of hope of surviving the night. He handed the mayor the red envelope with a trembling hand.

"Jared Cronin, of 542 Mountain Range Road, *you* are this year's selected recipient. In one hour, all of these people standing in front of you will no longer be your friends and family. Not until dawn tomorrow. Do not take it personally, son. We thank you for your selfless sacrifice to keep this town safe."

Selfless? Like I have a damn choice.

As the mayor continued rambling, Jared zoned out, thinking about where he'd go first. He scanned the area behind the crowd, observing the buildings that lined Main Street. Ms. Hendrix had said to consider places they wouldn't think to look. To start close by when everyone else would be searching the woods. It was a good thought, one that could possibly buy him more time if nobody spotted him hiding in town. He just couldn't bring himself to believe that starting out in the open was his best option. His attention came back to the herd of residents with determined faces staring at him as if he were a witch about to be burned at the stake. He found Shawn, who refused to make eye contact, instead staring straight at the ground, his skin a sickly pale tone. Then he came to Ms. Hendrix, who technically didn't even need to partake in the hunt with her perpetual immunity. The look in her eyes was different. She held his gaze. Slowly

—so slightly it was almost imperceptible—she nodded toward the town hall.

What is she trying to tell me? And why is she risking her immunity by helping, even if it isn't obvious what she's saying?

The bell blasted through the town, snapping Jared out of his thoughts. With each reverberating *dong*, the weight of its importance struck Jared like a hammer to the head. It was time. There was no more planning, no more having his parents try to calm him. His mom wept and grabbed him in an embrace, squeezing so tight that Jared thought she might actually kill him by force before he even got the chance to run. His dad walked up and touched foreheads with him, holding in his sobs to appear strong on the outside, but Jared knew he was a mess internally.

"You can do this. And you need to go now. Use all the time you have, Jared."

Without another word, Jared pried his mom's arms from their tight embrace and met her bloodshot eyes.

"I'm so sorry, honey. We love you."

Jared fought back his own tears, and he didn't say a word. If he did, he knew he would have a meltdown right here in front of the entire town, fall to the grass until his hour was up, and then they would all just kill him together. Jared tightened his backpack straps. His mother sobbed. His father clenched his jaw. He turned his back to the crowd . . .

And ran.

He didn't look back. But he felt them watching. Counting the minutes. Waiting to hunt.

PART FOUR
SCHOOL'S OUT FOR THE SUMMER:
ONE YEAR PRIOR

Jared and Shawn tore up the hill on their bikes, legs burning. School was officially out, and they had been planning all year on heading to their hideout, the "Dude Cave," to celebrate with some liquor and nudie magazines. Shawn had swiped the porn from his dad's stash under the mattress. The covers were permanently imprinted with square indents—silent proof of their hiding spot.

The boys had spent every weekend throughout the school year working on the hideout deep within the woods. It was a secret they kept to themselves. They built through snow, rain, and blistering heat. Nothing—not weather, school, or their parents—would stop them from finishing the Dude Cave.

As they passed the entrance to the park, Jared scanned the area to make sure nobody was watching them, curious to see what the two young boys were getting themselves into. Jared was sleeping over at Shawn's house, and the boys had plans to complete the finishing touches on the fort, solidifying it for a summer full of fun.

"Let's hide our bikes in the bushes up here and walk through the thicket," Jared said.

Shawn nodded and hopped off his bike, walking it down into the ditch and up the embankment heading into the forest. Jared followed, trudging through dense bushes and dropping his bike next to Shawn's, where they then covered their fallen soldiers with branches. While there was no trail within a mile, they knew the area well. Both agreed that they needed to mark trees leading to their spot but to do it discreetly so nobody would notice should they randomly veer off a path and get lost. Or worse, find it on Mail Day and destroy it. While neither of them spoke of Mail Day while building it, Jared had a feeling Shawn thought the same thing: it would make the perfect hiding spot if one of them was selected to be the hunted in the future.

The boys spent the better part of an hour trekking through the forest, following their hidden markings.

"You think anyone would ever see these marks we made?" Shawn asked.

"Eh, it's all about our system, right? Like they might see a mark on one of the trees and think it looks strange, but we marked each differently. I think we're safe. We can stash whatever the hell we want in this place," Jared said, laboring the words through rough terrain.

"Dude, you sound like you just jizzed your pants. You good?"

"Shut up, ass. I jizzed in your mom last night."

Shawn faked a gag and shook his head. "You're sick," he said, then continued walking.

Their markings were small designs, a logo they had

created in art class that became their identification out in these woods. A capital *S* with a *C* nuzzled into the top curve of the *S*. It stood for the first letters of their last names together—Spears and Cronin. They marked it at different heights—some high, some low—careful to place them in locations not easily visible should someone continue in the same direction for too long.

Up ahead, Jared spotted the fallen tree that indicated they were close. A tall pine that had fallen and somehow avoided hitting any others on the way down. They used the tip of the tree as a makeshift compass, aligning it to point in the direction of their hideout. Out here, the sun struggled to provide much light, but that was okay. It meant less attention on their area. Finally, they came to a cluster of smaller fallen trees, and Jared smiled.

"This is so fucking cool."

"I told my mom we'd be back for dinner. She's ordering pizza from Brookside," Shawn said.

"Nice!" The thought of a fresh cheese pizza had Jared's stomach rumbling. Thankfully, they brought snacks to hold them over. Jared approached the top of a fallen tree and grabbed hold of the tip. "I'll go down first, then hold open the door so you can climb in."

Both boys lifted up on the tree, which in turn not only pulled the tree off the ground, but also a four-foot-wide sheet of plywood with it that they had nailed on the underside of the trunk, creating a secret door. A hollow space opened beneath them—a six-by-four-foot underground bunker. Enough light forced its way in to reveal the supplies they had been storing for months like a couple of squirrels about to go into hibernation. Comic books, baseball cards, some small nips of alcohol that Jared had stolen from his parents' collection in the pantry. It was a teen's dream space, and it was all theirs.

Jared hopped in and pulled the lantern light from his backpack. He snapped the power on, blasting the dark space with illumination. Next, he grabbed the thick tree limb they had stored inside to use as a makeshift doorstop. He stood it up straight, wedging one end on the floor and the other to hold open the door a few feet to make sure they would have no issues getting out and would get plenty of fresh air circulating inside.

Shawn looked around to make sure nobody was nearby, then hopped down inside as well. Posters of their favorite movies and sports teams decorated the small walls. In the corner they had a plastic bin that had three drawers where they stored snacks, utensils, and the pocketknife Shawn's grandfather had given him for Christmas the previous year.

"So, what should we do first? Want to drink some of those nips?" Jared asked.

Shawn shrugged, still adjusting to the makeshift bunker. Jared grabbed the small bottles from the plastic bin and passed one to Shawn. After twisting the caps off, they tapped them together in a voiceless "Cheers" and swallowed the liquor. Jared's insides immediately burned. He squinted as his eyes watered, holding back a cough. He didn't understand why adults liked drinking so much.

"Holy shit. This stuff is awful," he said.

"Not mine. Tastes like FireBall candy," Shawn said.

They decided not to drink any more, unsure of what it would do to their bodies with it being their first time. Shawn pulled out one of the *Playboy* magazines and passed it to Jared with a smile on his face.

"Feast your eyes on these tits."

Jared pushed away the burning sensation in his stomach and opened the magazine. Sheer perfection. The warmth of the liquor began to relax him. His body felt almost numb in a way, and while the taste was disgusting, he now saw the appeal in drinking it. It wasn't about the taste, it was about how it made you feel.

"Does your dad spank it to these?" Jared asked out of the blue after scrolling through a few pages.

"*Eww*, fucking gross. I didn't even think of that. Imagine if you're touching the page he was looking at while doing it."

Jared threw the magazine into the corner as if it was covered in thousands of tiny bugs. Shawn laughed and tossed his as well.

"What should we do now?" Shawn asked.

"I don't know. Let's just hang in here. So damn cool."

"Hey . . . you think this would be a good hiding spot on Mail Day? Like, do you think anyone would find it and use it? Maybe we should hide our supplies somewhere else."

"Jesus, man. Don't say that. We can't talk about hiding spots with each other. What if one of us gets picked next year? Keep that shit to yourself."

The buzz was hitting full force now, and Jared wondered if Shawn felt the same. Based on his burning red cheeks, Jared assumed he did.

"Marty Devlin told me he heard there's dead zones around town. Where They can't hear anything. He says it's how Ms. Hendrix and Wes Tremblay survived. They found a dead zone and had help communicating with others. Of course, neither of them would ever admit that."

"Why would you believe anything "Farty Marty" says? That tool claims he saw Bigfoot roaming around the campground one summer. Said he was in the bathroom taking a dump and saw the hairy foot walking beneath the stall door."

Shawn laughed. "Yeah, true. It was probably just your mom's foot he saw."

Jared punched his friend and they both laughed again.

Dead zones. Could that really be a thing? Were there places where we could be safe from whoever is in charge of Mail Day?

It was something to consider for sure. Still, Jared didn't feel comfortable talking about any of this, even out in the woods with nobody within miles of them. He also let his mind consider the Dude Cave as a possible place to retreat to if needed. When they set out to build it, neither of the boys had discussed that scenario. As far as Jared knew, they were building it for fun, something to help pass the summer days and forget about what awaited the town each year. Maybe subconsciously they were creating this space with the true intention of it being buried inside of them all along.

"I know we can't talk about this stuff. But one last thing. If one of us ever gets picked . . . we have to make a pact right here and now. A blood oath," Shawn said.

Jared furrowed his brow, considering where Shawn was going with this.

"What do you mean, a 'blood oath'? We're not in some stupid cult, Shawn. You're kidding, right?"

Shawn let out a half-ass laugh and shimmied over to the container in the corner. He opened the middle drawer and pulled out his pocketknife. "I'm serious, man. If either of us gets picked on Mail Day, we need to agree right now to do anything we can to help the other one. Fuck this town, dude. All I care about is you and my family, and sometimes they're a distant second place."

Jared shook his head, hesitant to do something so stupid. They had been warned every year about what happens to those who don't follow the rules. He had no desire to put his family in danger.

"I don't know, dude. That . . . that's too dangerous. What if they came for our families anyway? We saw what happened to others."

"The way I look at it, if one of us is selected, I'd rather die than kill my best friend. We'll both be eligible for the first time next year. We know that increases the odds of being chosen. If you were picked . . . I couldn't do it. I'd purposely hunt in places I know you won't go. I'd—"

"Shut up, Shawn. Don't keep saying this stuff out loud. We never know who can hear us."

"They tell us we're always being listened to because they want to scare us. Like saying Santa won't deliver gifts if you're awake. Or that dragonflies will sew your mouth shut if you swear."

"That's just your mom who says that. Nobody else has ever heard such a stupid thing."

"I'm *serious*, Jared. Nobody can hear us out here. Watch." Shawn moved to the edge of the box and poked his head out the small opening. "Hey, assholes! The ones who are in charge of this stupid fucking town! I won't kill my friend! You hear me? And he won't kill me neither! Mail Day can suck my dick!"

Jared had heard enough. He yanked Shawn back down into the hole, swallowing a lungful of fear as he did.

"Are you fucking drunk or something? That's just asking for trouble, you moron!"

Shawn smirked and shrugged. He popped the blade out

on his pocketknife, bringing the tip to his palm. "No matter what happens . . . I won't kill you."

Before Jared could stop him, Shawn dug the blade into his palm, dragging it slow enough to leave a mark. Blood welled in the dim light. Shawn winced, but all in all, he handled it like a champ. When he was done, he held the butt of the knife out toward Jared.

"Your turn."

"I'm not doing it, you crazy bastard!"

He meant it. Jared had no intention of making himself bleed. Shawn must have sensed this because he held up his palm for Jared to see, and even in the shadows, it was clear what Shawn had carved into his skin. It was their logo, the same one they carved into all the trees on the way out here.

"I won't make you do anything you don't want to. But remember what we said. No matter what, we would be there for each other. So, if you really meant that, Jared, take it."

Jared didn't remember reaching for the knife, only that it was suddenly in his hand. For a moment, he just stared at the blade, trying to talk himself out of doing something so stupid. But Shawn was his best friend. They had a relationship closer than many brothers could even match. Jared exhaled and pressed the blade into his palm. The pain was sharp, fleeting. But the mark . . .

that would last forever.

Part Five
The Final Hour

Jared ran until his legs burned and his lungs begged for air. The countdown hadn't even started yet, but he needed a break. If he was going to make it through the night—hell, even just the morning—he needed to recalibrate. He found a section of broken-down cars, beaten and worn, the way he himself felt. It was one thing to discuss strategy with his parents throughout the year and another to put it into action. The simple things became challenging. Remembering basic instinctual tasks was a struggle.

Digging into his pocket, Jared pulled out his watch and fought back the bile when he discovered almost twenty minutes had already passed. In forty minutes, the town would come hunting. He set his backpack down and leaned against the trunk of a rusted-out Ford Mustang. Ms. Hendrix had nodded toward the town hall; he was certain of it. When he left the town common, Jared considered looping around the town and coming to the back side of the building, but the thought of all the residents being only feet away while he tried to hide scared him too much to risk it.

He turned his hand over and stared at his palm, at the scar he had carved into his skin last summer. Would Shawn really do anything to help him? Nobody else in town would know to look for the Dude Cave. If he could truly trust Shawn, that spot made the most sense. At the very least, he could start the day there and hopefully cut out a few hours before anyone got close. He knew that during this hour, the town would be discussing strategy. Pairing groups and assigning routes for them to track. Instructing loved ones to gather at the most likely places he would have gone first.

No matter how much he trusted Shawn, their hideout felt like too much of a risk . . . at least to start the day. Now that he was in this position, he realized why the woods were the most common places to find the recipients. He felt so naked out here in the open, as if everyone could see him no matter where he went. Nobody could see him here. But he still felt their eyes—thousands of them, watching, waiting.

The day would likely go off the rails, but it still felt important to have a rough plan in mind. He had to think of what the townsfolk would most likely do once the clock tower rang out again. A large portion of the residents would go to the woods, spreading out to create a wide radius as they searched the forest like they were a crew trying to solve a cold case. The next most popular spot would be the gravel pit on the far end of town, followed by any of the abandoned buildings where so many had been discovered roaming in past years.

The junkyard was as good a place as any to start. While some of the hunters would more than likely come here, it wouldn't be at the top of their list. Jared decided this was the place he'd wait until he moved on to the Dude Cave. He picked up his bag and walked farther into the junkyard, seeking out a place that wouldn't be obvious yet would hide him from the naked eye. He passed a section of old stoves, washers, and dryers and considered climbing into one of those and hiding himself. It was something to ponder but instead, he decided to keep going, hoping there would be a better alternative.

Next, he stumbled upon scrap metal and junk parts. Even if he could lift the heavy stuff enough to hide, he thought there was as good a chance of getting a cut and dying of tetanus as there was an angry mob slitting his throat. He needed to keep going. The deeper into the junkyard he went, the more he wondered if this was a big mistake. As if he needed another reason to think that, the bell at the town hall sounded, echoing through Pembroke.

It was time for the hunt.

Jared's heart rattled in his chest, his breath coming in heavy bursts. He picked up speed, running around a bend full of junk metal, then came to a crowded lot of old vehicles. Some were stacked on top of one another, while others were folded like an accordion. Some of the cars were so old that Jared thought they must be from before his parents were even born, while others were very recent. Recognizing a handful as the vehicles of past recipients of the envelope, he felt a sudden knot tighten in his chest. It was as if those people were erased from the record books, hidden from the outside world and meant to be forgotten forever. He refused to be another name scratched off Pembroke's history—another body tossed into the junkyard of forgotten victims.

He wanted to be in a place before anyone got close enough to hear him moving stuff around to hide. Deep in the belly of a car pile, he spotted an old camper that was folded in half at the center of the roof yet intact enough to climb into. It was as good a spot as any to disappear for a while.

Without hesitation, Jared sprinted to the pile of vehicles and jumped up on the hood of an old Chevy truck. He climbed down the other side, careful not to step awkwardly and roll his ankle on any scrap metal. The window on the driver's-side door of the camper was crushed, shards of jagged glass poking out from the frame like shark teeth ready to chomp down on him if he got close. He took his backpack off and slid it across the open window, clearing the broken glass as best he could, then tossed the bag into the passenger seat before climbing in himself.

Once he was inside, Jared was immediately overcome with relief. Any hunter would have to search long and hard to find him in this place. He sat in the driver's seat for a moment collecting his thoughts. The windshield was caved in, a spider-webbed blanket curving down to almost touch him. Through the glass, all Jared saw was the crushed metal of more vehicles, with only a tiny space giving him access to see the junkyard beyond. In any other situation, it would be suffocating, but right now, it made him feel safe.

He realized that he couldn't stay in the seat, though, because anyone walking by might spot him sitting there if they happened to glance over. Behind him, Jared searched for an easy path to the rear of the camper where nobody would see him. Where the roof folded in, there were sharp daggerlike tips of metal that extended a few feet down. He'd have to crawl beneath them to get into the back.

After resting for a moment, Jared squatted between the front seats and slid his bag under the folded roof. He then crawled beneath, careful to avoid getting cut along the way. Once he had shimmied through enough, he pulled himself up and discovered the sleeping quarters of the camper. He couldn't believe his luck. There was a chance he could spend the entire day and night here and not even need to go on the run. The inside smelled of mildewed furniture, like a couch with a *FREE* sign that had been left on the side of the road through a thunderstorm and gotten soaked to the core.

Jared sat on the couch that lined the wall and grabbed his water from his bag. He knew he needed to ration it, but took a massive gulp anyway, then put it back in the backpack. At this point, he knew his parents would be searching for him. They wouldn't want to, but they had no choice. As scared as he was and as mad as he was at them, whether it was fair or not, he also felt bad for them. He couldn't imagine what they must be feeling as they walked through town with other residents, searching for their son with the intention of killing him.

And then to make matters worse, once he was dead, the town would move on like nothing happened, leaving his parents to grieve alone. The residents of Pembroke treated the curse on the town like a strange pain in the stomach that they knew was cancer, but if they just ignored it, the pain would go away, and they could never get that true death sentence.

The camper's outdated interior décor led him to believe it must be at least twenty years old. Wooden panel walls, flower wallpaper above the sink, it felt like a capsule of another time. He noticed one of the drawers beneath the sink open slightly and got up to check it out. There was some rusted silverware and mouse droppings scattered within. He considered taking one of the knives for self-defense. One of the rules was that the recipient couldn't take weapons from their own home, but if they found something in the wild, it was fair game. While killing one of the hunters was forbidden, hurting them to defend yourself was well within the rules.

He opened the second drawer, again finding a ridiculous amount of mouse shit mixed with chewed-up paper and other materials the rodents must have used to try and form a nest in the camper. As he was about to shut the drawer, he spotted a map. He pulled it out, shook it to remove the droppings, then unfolded and studied it. It was a map of the town, but it was aged. The pages stained with water and rodent piss. Jared found it odd that someone would've had a map of the town they lived in hidden in their camper. Was this from an outsider? Or maybe a past recipient who used the map to look for places to hide? This made him wonder if someone had previously discovered this exact spot to disappear. Suddenly, he didn't feel so safe.

The map had locations circled, lines drawn, and scribbles that Jared couldn't make out due to fading over the years. He felt the map might help later and shoved it into his bag. He spent the next few minutes checking the cabinets and the rest of the drawers, deciding there wasn't anything else of use. Then he walked over to the mini fridge, somehow unharmed during the destruction. It was partially open, revealing a dark space within. Jared opened the door and jumped back. Inside, a family of dead mice lay in a mound of hollowed carcasses and dried insides.

They had clearly been there a long time, as the bodies had absorbed into one another, looking more like a creature from *The Thing* than a pack of harmless mice. *This is what happens when the family sticks together. Instead of some of them escaping and living their lives, they all suffered a miserable death of starvation and rotted away.* He couldn't help but think his family would suffer the same fate if his parents tried to save him. In a way, he couldn't blame them for following the rules.

Jared slammed the door shut and decided that was enough exploring for the time being. He sat back on the couch and listened, wondering when the first sign of residents getting close would come. From this spot, he still had a small space in the windshield to watch through, although the warped glass distorted what little area he could see. He sat in the dark, keeping his eyes glued forward.

Sounds from somewhere behind the camper finally jarred Jared from his trance—muffled voices and footsteps approaching from the other end of the junkyard. Even though he remained hidden, Jared couldn't help but feel his veins go cold as ice. He had managed to go an hour without disturbance, but it only felt like five minutes had passed. It reminded him that he could not let his guard down.

The hunters were now close enough that he heard certain words. Whoever it was, they were just talking like they were out in the woods tracking a deer. He couldn't see them yet, but it sounded like they stopped right on the other side of the camper.

"This place is a gold mine for someone to hide. I say we check every damn one of these vehicles," a woman said.

"That would take the entire fucking day. You really wanna waste that much time out here when the rest of the town is out searching the more likely spots?" a man asked.

"Fine. But let's at least check some of the cars he could crawl into."

Shit!

Jared hoped the camper was hidden enough that they would move past it without noticing. He crouched lower, hoping that would offer more protection. The voices stopped talking, and then they came into view through the front windshield, facing the other direction. One of them was Spencer Oswalt, the town barber. Jared didn't recognize the woman, but he assumed it was the man's wife. Spencer twirled his ax like he was itching to use it. The woman's wooden spear looked freshly sharpened—she was planning to make the killing slow.

Jesus Christ, would they really try to kill me with those things? Like I'm some evil vampire trying to suck the life out of this town?

The couple picked through the crushed vehicles on the other side, opening doors and trunks. Mr. Oswalt cursed at something, then raised the ax and slammed it down into the trunk of a car. The metal-on-metal sound sent goose-flesh across Jared's arms. He pictured the ax driving into his neck, leaving his head hanging by a thread of muscle and skin.

The man raised the ax again, prepared to strike the car, when his wife put her hand on his forearm to stop him.

"What? What do you want?" he snapped.

"Look . . ."

The woman pointed to the dirt path, and Jared felt a sinking feeling in the pit of his stomach.

She was pointing to his footprints, which led them right to the camper. Even from his hiding spot, Jared saw the smile on the barber's face. They stopped what they were doing and marched toward the pile of vehicles covering the camper. Jared grabbed one of the knives from the silverware drawer and gripped it tight. A place that felt like such a great spot to hide now felt like a death trap. If they discovered him, there was only one way in and out. They wouldn't be able to kill him with their weapons if he remained in here, but one of them could easily guard the camper while the other ran to town to let everyone know.

"Oh, Jared, buddy . . . we appreciate you making this a short day's work for us. And for giving us immunity. You might as well come out from wherever you're hiding so you don't have to suffer," the barber said.

They got close enough that they were no longer visible, located somewhere along the side of the camper. Everything returned to silence, but their footsteps lightly pattered on the ground nearby. Jared held his breath, praying for something to distract them, to take them on a different path and leave him alone. A brutal *CRACK* split the air—the ax head punched through the camper wall, stopping inches from Jared's face. He screamed before he could stop himself.

The blade disappeared, then reentered a few feet closer. Jared had to do something, or they were going to cut the whole fucking wall off and have full access to him. He climbed over the junk littered on the floor, crawled back to the driver's seat—

And came face-to-face with the woman.

"He's here!" she hollered, then raised the long spear and attempted to impale him through the window.

He dodged the sharp point, watching it move past his head and into the cushion of the passenger seat.

"It's nothing personal, Jared. You know that. Come on out of there," the barber said from over the woman's shoulder.

He was trapped. The only escape was through the window these psychos currently blocked. Unless . . .

Jared jumped over to the passenger seat, out of reach while the woman continued trying to pry her spear free from the seat. He leaned back and kicked the blanket of glass caving in from the windshield, squinting to avoid any shards that might fall his way. The windshield lifted and fell back in place but dipped a little more than before. He kicked it again, watching the webbing spread across the center of the glass. The third kick shattered the section in front of him. He immediately stood in a crouch and again used his bag to clear some space to crawl through.

"Stop him!" Spencer Oswalt yelled.

"I'm trying! I can't get this out of the seat!"

"Then move out of my way," the barber said, shoving her to the side.

Jared took advantage of the bickering and climbed through the windshield as the ax came crashing into the camper. Maybe it was his imagination, but Jared could have sworn the blade of the ax just missed his left foot.

Now on the hood, Jared was doused in panic. Where would he go? There was metal on metal above and below him, with only a small opening to crawl through. The ax struck one of the crushed vehicles above him, trying to break through with a loud *clang* that reverberated through the entire mass of steel. Sparks flew. Oswalt yelled. He was deranged, dead set on getting to the target by any means necessary.

The ax stopped striking, and then Jared heard a conversation again. There was a third man coming to help them. The voices escalated, but Jared couldn't hear what they were saying through the wall of cars. He had to risk climbing out and making a run for it. Turning onto his stomach, he crawled toward the small opening, feeling sharp metal fangs digging into his back as he went. He continued, using only his upper body as his legs had no room to move. Finally, he reached the hole and stopped to listen.

It sounded like the third man was arguing with the barber and the woman. When immunity was on the line, it was easy to see why things could get heated between the hunters. Jared needed to take advantage of the bickering. He pulled himself through the hole, falling to the ground below, barely missing a rusty bumper with sharp edges facing upward ready to penetrate his flesh.

He sat up, ready to defend himself if needed, and saw Maxine Kaine's dad holding a pistol. Only he wasn't aiming it at Jared. He had it pointed at Spencer Oswalt. The barber held his hands up in surrender while the woman stood frozen in fear.

"Listen, Kaine. This is a terrible fucking mistake, and you know it. If you mess with the rules, we could all be in danger," Spencer said. His tone was calm, but it was drenched in uneasiness.

Mr. Kaine looked like a walking corpse. His skin sagged, his glasses fogged from sweat. He had vanished after killing Maxine, and now . . . now he had returned like a ghost with unfinished business. Rumors spread across town that he had committed suicide, skipped town, or even locked himself inside his home. Here he was, in the flesh, but he might as well have been dead.

"I don't care anymore. About this town. About any of you . . . selfish assholes. I lost my wife. Then I put a bullet in my own daughter's skull, all for *you*. And what did Pembroke do? They went back to their *fucking lives* like she'd never even existed. Until next year. Until the next unlucky soul. Look at this. He's a boy, hasn't even graduated high school yet. And you're all out here trying to cut him up with a fucking ax. I'm done with it. All of it," Mr. Kaine said, pointing the gun at Oswalt.

"Kaine . . . don't do something stupid. You know it's much bigger than any of—"

BANG!

Spencer Oswalt staggered backward, clutching his face. He let out a garbled scream—the sound of a man drowning in his own blood.

He dropped to his knees, blinking his one remaining eye in confusion before faceplanting onto the dirt. Jared's ears rang, he dropped to the ground out of instinct, then looked up to see if Mr. Kaine had really shot the barber. The woman shrieked and lunged, but she only made it three steps before the gun found her.

BANG!

Her cheek exploded, splattering red mist into the air. Her body spun from the force and Kaine pulled the trigger a third time.

BANG!

The final bullet entered the back of her head. She dropped hard, landing next to the barber.

Jared couldn't believe what he was witnessing. He took panicked breaths, unsure of what to do. Mr. Kaine stood there for a moment, staring at the two bodies he had just disposed of. A major—if not *the* most important—rule of Mail Day had just been broken. Jared had no idea what this meant for anyone in town. All he knew was that he was still alive.

Mr. Kaine snapped out of it and turned his attention to Jared on the ground.

"They made me kill my Maxine. I have nothing left. I'm sorry for Pembroke. I'm sorry for you, son. I'm sorry for what will happen."

Jared wanted to say something, but his lips were sealed shut with fear. Mr. Kaine wept, then lifted the gun. Jared raised his hands to guard his face, ready to be the final victim of this deranged lunatic. But he didn't aim the gun at Jared. A twisted sob tore from Kaine's throat—anger, grief, *relief.* Then he jammed the gun into his own mouth—

And pulled the trigger.

BANG!

His body jerked as brain matter splattered against a rusted truck hood behind him. He hit the dirt, *finally free.*

Three dead bodies surrounded Jared. He was in shock, unable to move. It wasn't until he realized the gunshots would draw attention that he forced himself to his feet. He looked around at the massacre, then toward the entrance of the junkyard. The residents who were close enough to hear the gunshots would come through there, making it too dangerous to backtrack. He put his backpack over his shoulders, then turned and ran deeper into the junkyard. He ran as fast as he could, for as long as he could, until he reached the fence surrounding the end of the property.

He assumed people would be close, if they weren't already here discovering the bodies of their friends. Would they think Jared was responsible? Did it even matter who was? He climbed the fence and disappeared into the forest that surrounded the land. A scream came from somewhere behind him, and he knew the bodies had been found. He kept running, ignoring the branches slapping his face as he weaved between trees, wondering what all of this meant for the town.

Part Six
A Storm Is Brewing

The sound of running water emerged from up ahead, letting Jared know he was approaching the river. It was a popular place for hunters to search, so Jared wasn't thrilled at the idea of heading in this direction. He wasn't exactly sure where he was, but if he had to guess, he thought he would eventually come out near the park.

What would happen to Pembroke now? Mr. Kaine didn't kill for *Jared*—he did it because this town stole everything from him. But did that even matter? Would the ones in charge punish everyone anyway? Would whoever controlled this sick and twisted curse see it as breaking the rules and torture Pembroke, even though the remaining residents still continued their hunt for him?

The trees thinned up ahead, presenting the running water that he'd heard for the last few minutes. Any moment now, a group of hunters could track him down and have their way with him. He stopped walking, scanning the surrounding area for anything that looked familiar. He and Shawn had trekked through much of these woods when seeking a place to build their Dude Cave, but none of this resembled any land they had traveled.

He considered walking along the edge until he came to a place he recognized, but the thought of staying close to the river didn't sit right with him. The water level wasn't too high at the moment, which was unusual for this time of year. During the hunt last year, the river was dangerously high thanks to plentiful rainfall in the days leading up to Mail Day. Jared decided crossing it was his best option, and then he would attempt to get to the Dude Cave and spend as much time there as he could. While it already felt like many hours had passed, in actuality it had only been a few, leaving plenty of daylight left to try and survive.

Jared sat on the ground and untied his shoes, then took them off along with his socks, and shoved them into the backpack. If he was going to cross through the water, he preferred not to have his feet soaked for the rest of the day. It was bad enough running for your life, doing it with damp feet was just unnecessary torture.

He stood and carefully climbed down the embankment to the rocky shore. The water was calming, a light trickle breaking up the silence. He stuck his foot in the river and immediately pulled it back out. The water was ice-cold, numbing his toes in an instant. *This is going to suck.* Cursing under his breath, he forced himself into the water, hoping it didn't get much deeper than his ankles. It only took a few steps in to have those hopes crushed. The water quickly rose to his knees, then his thighs, before leveling off. Jared was grateful it didn't reach his waist, or his nuts, for that matter. As it was, they wanted to shrivel up inside themselves.

The mild current weakly pulled at him, but it wasn't strong enough to scare him. He carefully stepped across the bottom, taking each step slowly to avoid cutting his feet on jagged rocks. When he reached the other side, he climbed up the embankment and sat down to catch his breath for a minute. Once he got his socks and shoes back on, he prepared to continue moving when he heard muffled voices coming from somewhere nearby.

For fuck's sake! Can I get one goddamn break?

He got to his feet and listened closely, determining that the voices were coming from the side across the water where he had started. He needed to put some distance between them before they realized he was close. And just like that, he was sprinting through the woods again. Hopefully the sounds from the water would block out the crunching leaves and branches beneath his panicked steps. Otherwise, he was putting a huge bullseye on himself. Every few minutes he stopped to catch his breath and listen for the pursuers, only hearing the normal sounds of the forest.

A loud rumble traveled across Pembroke like crackling thunder. Jared didn't remember hearing about any storms approaching. Before he entered the woods, the sky had been bright and sunny.

Eventually the forest thinned again, and when Jared got close enough to the tree line to observe the area beyond, he was relieved to recognize where he was. That relief was short-lived once he spotted a few women—likely moms of kids he went to school with, though it was hard to tell with them a few hundred yards away. Had they seen him? Their demeanor was far too calm for a group of savages who just spotted their prize. Behind the women, Jared saw the tower of the metal factory. Smoke billowed up through the clouds, a mix of gray and white that suffocated the sky and blocked out the sun.

If he was near the factory, it meant he had to travel west to reach the Dude Cave. Right now, though, he had to just get out of there undetected. Then he wanted to study the map he'd discovered. First, he needed to assess the situation. He knew there were hunters behind him, but they hadn't crossed the river. In front of him, the women continued moving closer.

Jared prepared to get moving again when his eyes were drawn back to the clouds. They continued to darken, creating a thick plume of smoke like the center of a house fire. He realized it wasn't just the smoke from the factory mixing with the clouds. There was something else forming *inside* the smog. He froze, mesmerized by the shapes molding together above. The women stopped walking and looked up as well, then one of them screamed. The swirling smoke twisted and coiled, pulling itself into a shape. Something massive. Something wrong. The air itself shuddered as it took form, towering over the buildings like a god of death.

"Oh . . . my . . . god," Jared whispered.

It couldn't be a coincidence that the rules had just been broken and now some monster was created out of thin air. It floated very high in the sky, its upper half now gaining more clarity, but its bottom half still diluted in the clouds. A face formed, revealing razor-sharp teeth followed by a set of eyes that were long and thin, filled in with an obsidian-like darkness.

The women hunters attempted to retreat, their cries audible even from such a far distance. The cloud stretched, creating an elongated arm that extended into a clawed hand the size of a car, which hung only a few feet above the group.

One of the women took off in a sprint as the other two ran for the closest building. The woman sprinting down the road looked over her shoulder and up at the cloud hand as it started to swoop toward her. She gasped—one final breath—before black talons tore through her spine and ripped out the other side. Her upper body peeled away in a spray of gore, leaving her legs standing for half a second before they collapsed like a puppet with its strings cut.

Jared fell backward onto his ass, covering his mouth to prevent fear-filled cries from escaping. The cloud monster wrapped around the lady's upper body and then launched her through the air. She was already dead, but the odd silence ended when her body slammed against the side of a brick building, turning to mush as it oozed down the wall, leaving a trail of gore and viscera in its wake.

The other two hunters were no longer visible, but Jared heard their panicked cries as they sought shelter from the monster. The thing's mouth opened wide again, letting out an audible roar that sounded like a distant bomb going off, explaining the random strike of what he'd presumed was thunder.

Jared couldn't believe this was happening. All the warnings, training, and preparation could never prepare him for the scene unfolding. The slideshow that the mayor forced the residents to watch every year was nothing compared to seeing this in real life. Because in those photos, the town only saw a set of still frames of the aftermath. Nobody lived to see it in action. There were rumors of how *They* kept the rules in place all these years, and he was now seeing it firsthand.

His eyes glued to the nightmare, he found himself unable to take advantage of this distraction. The cloud monster's body darkened to near-black smoke, and the eyes let off a faint glow. Just as Jared convinced himself to get moving, he heard a distant shouting closer to the factory. He squinted through the smoke and clouds, spotting an army of residents sprinting toward the scene. Jared wondered why anyone in their right mind would come *toward* this instead of running as far away as possible, but then he got his answer.

Mayor Thompson led the crowd, which was made up of at least ten residents that Jared could see. The mayor was shouting something, waving his hands back and forth as if trying to garner the attention of the monstrosity in the sky.

"Stop! Please, I beg of you! We're following the rules. It wasn't us helping the boy. It was . . . it was Andrew Kaine! He took his own life after. Surely, you saw that!"

Mayor Thompson stopped running as the rest of the residents caught up, all of them panting and out of breath. The face in the sky shifted, staring down at the crowd. Jared spotted Mr. Roberts with his dog, Harper, along with a few others he recognized from around town. Then he spotted Shawn's dad, who was typically a nice man and treated Jared like a second son, but right now he wasn't a dad. He was a hunter, and his eyes flitted around like a crazed lunatic.

The whole group stood behind the mayor, awaiting instruction. It was clear they were conscripted by Thompson as he made his way to this end of town.

"Please . . . we'll *fix* this. We'll find the boy and *make him pay.* You already took one of us—*isn't that enough?* We swore an oath to you, and we have lived by it for over a century."

Jared had always feared the town. But *this*—watching its leader beg to something inhuman and knowing that Mayor Thompson would sell them all out if it meant saving himself —was worse than anything.

The cloud monster soared over them, staring down at the

mayor as he got on his knees and begged. The residents followed suit—including Shawn's dad—and the entire clan of hunters were now lined up like a group of religious zealots who took their faith to the extreme. Only Harper, the German shepherd, refused to comply. Instead, the dog bared his teeth and growled at the cloud, his hackles raised.

"*Sit*, Harper!" Mr. Roberts snapped.

The dog hesitated, his growls turning to whimpers, but eventually he listened to his master and sat by his side. The townsfolk froze in silence as they awaited what was next to come.

The smoke face shot down, stretching to get within a few feet of the group. They all gasped. With it being this close, Jared now saw its features with more clarity. Water dripped from its mouth, looking like drooling precipitation. The face moved along the line of residents, pausing before each as if it was observing them. Finally, it stopped in front of Mayor Thompson, who continued to mutter something too quietly for Jared to hear. The smoke inched closer to the mayor, leading to a coughing fit as it engulfed his face.

"Please! I work so hard to make sure they all stay in line; you know I do! If you must . . . take one as a sacrifice that *They* will accept. But not me. This town needs me to remain orderly!"

Of course. That coward. He'd throw anyone under the bus, just as long as it wasn't him.

The apparent united front of the crowd ended with that statement from the mayor. All of them began screaming at one another in a state of panic. Jared's shock was wearing off, and he realized *now* was his chance to escape. He didn't want to see what happened next anyway. One dead body was enough for his lifetime. Jared forced himself to move. The screams behind him curdled his blood, but he didn't look back. He couldn't. The Dude Cave was waiting. He just had to make it there before the whole town burned.

As he weaved between trees, another thundering bellow erupted behind him, followed by multiple screams. He didn't have it in him to turn around and see if the mayor's plea to take another sacrifice was fulfilled. He needed to get to the Dude Cave. There, he would study the map, eat some food to fuel his depleting energy, and come up with a plan.

PART SEVEN
THE DUDE CAVE

After backtracking through the woods and getting close enough to the river to hear the chattering of hunters on the other side of the water, Jared traveled in the direction of the Dude Cave. On a normal day, the trek from the factory took about an hour. Jared was running it in half that time. His lungs burned, his legs screamed, but he couldn't stop—not yet. His heartbeat pounded in his ears, drowning out the forest. Every step felt like moving through quicksand, but stopping meant death. On a few occasions, he had to rest and hide behind a tree as residents passed by on the street. He wasn't being careful enough, but they all appeared to be distracted by the commotion near the factory. He couldn't blame them. This was uncharted territory for Pembroke, at least since he had been alive.

When he felt he had ventured far enough away from the group of hunters, Jared approached the road, stopping just shy of the tree line to peer out for any stragglers. The coast was clear. He quickly crossed the road and entered the woods on the other side. From here, he would need to walk a few miles through the dense foliage before he reached his destination. He was both grateful and annoyed by the thickness of the underbrush through the first twenty feet or so leading into the woods. There would be no sign of footprints leading to the forest, but trudging through it was a pain in the ass.

He knew that as the day went on, and the residents of Pembroke felt an overwhelming sense of desperation, the hunt would get more intense. Right now, there was still plenty of time to find the recipient. It didn't mean that most weren't taking it seriously, but when the townsfolk got desperate, they would go to unethical measures to find him. For example, Harper was the only dog the mayor allowed to sniff out recipients. They didn't want to have an accident where an untrained mutt killed the selected, preventing someone from receiving future immunity. As day turned to night, though, all bets were off. The hounds would be unleashed to track him down. Also, most residents traveled on foot during the day, feeling it was easiest to find the hunted when they had access to all their senses, methodically taking their time checking every inch of the town. When the sun went down, many of them would take their vehicles, ATVs, and bikes to cover more ground.

This all made the Dude Cave the perfect place to hide. There were no trails to traverse on wheels. The dogs may eventually find him out here, but it was well off the beaten path. Plus, one of the items he and Shawn kept in the cubby underground was a can of bear spray. Shawn's dad was an avid hunter—of wild game at any other time of the year—and the boys had overheard him talking with his buddies about how bear spray messed with the hunting dogs they brought to track their prey. Shawn snuck a can when they had spent the better part of a week stocking up on random supplies during the summer.

Jared instinctively looked at his palm and the scar he had carved during that time, hoping the pact he and Shawn made to help one another if either was selected on Mail Day would bear fruit when the moment called for it. Shawn had no choice but to hunt for him now that he was of age to do so. If the outraged adults in town pushed Shawn hard enough, asking where his best friend would go, hopefully their hideout that they'd spent countless hours building would stay out of Shawn's mouth. There were plenty of other spots he could lead them to that wouldn't be a lie.

Would I really do the same for him? If they pressed hard enough—if they threatened my family—would I break? No. Never.

Jared spotted the first carving on one of the trees, telling him he was heading in the right direction. His pant legs were still damp, rubbing and irritating his skin. If crossing the river saved his life, it was well worth the inconvenience. After following the secret path, the tree pointing in the direction of the hideout came into view.

Not much farther. Get in, grab the bear spray, then get situated for a (hopefully) long stay.

Ever since the nightmare in the street, things had gone pretty smooth. Almost *too* smooth, considering what he had already been through over the course of the morning. Finally, he came to the fallen pine tree. The Dude Cave. Jared exhaled, but his body refused to relax. He scanned the woods

—twice—his skin crawling with the feeling that someone, somewhere was watching.

He grabbed hold of the tree nailed to the makeshift door, hoping he was strong enough to lift it himself. He and Shawn had never been here without the other, so they never practiced opening and shutting the heavy door solo. Jared bent his knees and pushed the plywood up with force. At first, he thought he wasn't able to get the door up all the way, that he'd wasted all this time coming here only to have to abort and go somewhere else. But he pushed with all the strength he had left, and the door lifted fully open.

After tossing his bag into the hole, Jared hopped inside and set the thick branch in place to hold the door ajar. He quickly crawled over to the cubby and pulled out the bear spray, then climbed out and prepared to douse the surrounding area. He read the instructions and was thankful he hadn't sprayed before doing so. The last thing he needed to do was make his space uninhabitable by suffocating himself. Instead, he made sure he was at least fifteen feet away from the Dude Cave, then sprayed the perimeter of the hideout. He was immediately hit with a spicy odor, then with the aftertaste of a sweet, chemical scent. His eyes watered, but if it kept the dogs away, it would all be worth it. Once he was done, he walked back to the hole and climbed inside.

A streak of fire exploded across his palm.

"Shit!"

Jared jerked back, cradling his hand as white-hot pain seared deep into his skin. His palm turned an angry red, the burn digging in like a thousand needles. With his good hand, Jared unzipped his bag and grabbed the water bottle and the extra shirt he had packed in case he got cold at night. He dumped some water on the shirtsleeve, then vigorously rubbed at his palm. It didn't help. He soaked the shirt some more, then wrapped it around his hand tightly. Whether the substance was scrubbed off or covering it from the fresh air did the trick, the pain finally dulled, though not completely. Jared had a feeling he would be constantly reminded of his dumb mistake for the rest of the day.

With the door still open a few feet, daylight bled into the wooden box, providing enough light to see inside without wasting the batteries in his flashlight. He decided he would leave the door open for now, helping him to hear any approaching hunters. The first hint of anyone getting close and he would shut himself in. With his hand now recovering, he sat back down against the wall and grabbed a cereal bar from his bag. While he ate it, he considered everything that had happened so far.

Mr. Kaine stopped those hunters from killing him, and within half an hour, that monster formed in the sky. So what the hell was it? Was it man-made? Was it some evil entity that watched over the town? Either way, it clearly wasn't a coinci-dence. Especially with the way Mayor Thompson communi-cated with it. He knew what it was. And he was willing to sacrifice not just Jared but anyone in town to save his own ass. The sounds Jared heard while fleeing the scene were nauseat-ing. He had no doubt that there was at least one more casu-alty, possibly more. He hoped Shawn's dad was left unharmed. He couldn't imagine his best friend losing his father; they were so close that it would break Shawn.

When he was done eating the cereal bar, Jared pulled the map out of his bag and unfolded it, looking it over thor-oughly for the first time. It wasn't just a map of Pembroke, there were markings on it: arrows, abbreviations, giant *X* marks, and more. Now that he had the time to really study it, he wanted to decipher what all of it meant. It reminded him of a giant treasure map one would see in a pirate movie, or something from an open world video game that told him what the next destination was.

"Where are you pointing to?" he asked while tracing the arrow with his index finger.

The writing was sloppy, hard to read. But he couldn't blame whoever wrote it if they were running for their lives while jotting stuff down. His finger traced the map. The area near the Dude Cave had a marking—two letters: *DC*. Jared's stomach flipped. It couldn't be. No one else knew what they called it. He tilted the paper, catching the faded indent of an older marking. Not *DC*. His breath hitched. It was *DZ*.

"Dead zone."

His heart hammered, and he quickly scanned the rest of the map and located multiple locations with the same two letters.

"Holy shit, it's true."

I don't know that. Who's to say this is a fact? What if it's just a guess? If it was someone who didn't survive, maybe they thought these places were dead zones and they were wrong.

It was a logical thought, one he hated himself for thinking when all he wanted was a bit of hope. Then he flipped the map over, and in the bottom left corner, he noticed four words written in microscopic letters.

Property of Wes Tremblay.

This map belonged to Wes. One of the only two survivors to ever live past Mail Day. Jared was giddy with excitement, something he didn't think he could feel in a situation like this. According to the map, there was a dead zone just a few miles east of the Dude Cave. If he could get there . . . Well, he wasn't sure what it would do for him. It felt like a big deal, but Jared knew hunters wouldn't give a damn about communicating with him. They only wanted to kill him and gain lifetime immunity.

Regardless, he would relish this small victory on a day when, historically, wins were few and far between. If he was forced to abandon the cave, he would attempt to head toward the first dead zone and hope to find a way to communicate with his parents. How, he had no idea. He didn't have a cell phone with him, and even if he found a way from his end, his parents weren't going to be in a dead zone themselves. What good would it do for him to talk with them if everything on their end was being monitored?

Another thing Jared had to worry about was Wes Tremblay. While it was true that survivors not only had future immunity from being selected and also didn't have to partake in the hunt anymore, Wes didn't care. He hunted every year and enjoyed it. To him, it was a sick game, and the town bit their tongue around him, but Jared had heard the rumblings. Wes Tremblay scared the residents of Pembroke. He knew how to survive, which meant he knew what it took for other recipients to survive. For all Jared knew, Wes might be checking each of the dead zones or even waiting it out, hiding in the foliage like a hunter sitting in a deer stand all day.

Jared considered taking a nap to regain some energy, but he knew sleeping was a lost cause. Any sounds, movements, odd scents, they all kept him on edge. Time moved slowly, inching closer toward surviving, yet still so far away. Just when he allowed himself to get comfortable, something shuffled in the bushes out of sight.

Shit.

Will they see the open door?

He had to risk shutting it. Quietly, he peered out,

watching for any sign of movement. There it was again, the sound of something traveling over the dry twigs and leaves, too far away to see. Jared quietly grabbed the branch holding the door open, setting it down gently on the fort floor. Then he eased the door down, bringing the box to complete darkness. He was immediately hit with a bout of panic, the air getting stuffy within seconds. Still, he needed to keep the door shut.

The steps got louder, closer.

If it was a group of hunters, they weren't talking. Jared hoped the bear spray would do its job if it was Mr. Roberts and his dog. How long had it been since he sprayed it? Was the smell so strong that a person would notice it? He didn't dare move an inch, and it wasn't until he finally allowed himself to shift slightly that he realized how tense his muscles were. He couldn't even see a foot in front of him, just pitch-black nothingness, as if he were floating in space with no stars. He waited well past the last time he heard movement nearby. When the forest returned to silence, Jared decided to risk a look outside. His breaths were coming in short, furious bursts. With a trembling hand, he lifted the door a few inches to peer out, scanning the space that was visible.

The woods were still. Too still. Jared held his breath. Then, a flicker of movement in the underbrush. A shadow. He gripped the door tighter, preparing to slam it shut when—

A face.

Shawn?

A momentary joy at seeing his best friend was quickly diminished when he realized Shawn might not be alone. They locked eyes with one another. Shawn raised his index finger to his mouth, begging his friend to remain quiet. He then pointed to a blind spot that Jared couldn't see. He didn't dare move, afraid that any sudden shift would give away his spot. Leaving the door open felt like a huge mistake, but he didn't want to lose sight of Shawn. The crunching of the nearby forest floor somewhere behind the cave told him otherwise. Shawn motioned to close the lid and go back into hiding, so that's what Jared did.

Again, he returned to darkness and waited. He waited for what felt like an eternity until he heard the mumbling of voices nearby. He pressed his ear to the wall and listened, trying to pick up on anything being said.

"Where . . . Shawn, you better not be hiding . . ."

"I'm not . . . I thought he might be out this way . . . . I promise."

Jared didn't hear much of the conversation, but he heard enough. Shawn had led some hunters—how many, Jared wasn't sure—out to these woods. His stomach dropped. His best friend had led them here? After everything? His pulse pounded, anger burning through him. Until he heard Shawn leading them *away*. He knew if he led them here, and they *didn't* find the Dude Cave, they were less likely to come back. Shawn led them here so that he could eventually steer them away permanently.

Whoever Shawn was talking to—an older woman by the sound of it—said, "Okay. Let's go. You better have some other ideas, kid."

They were leaving. A sudden panic hit Jared, and he scurried to the cubby and pulled out a notebook the boys had stashed. As quickly as he could, he wrote a note, hoping he could get it to Shawn without anyone noticing.

This is a stupid idea. Shawn just saved my ass, and I'm going to risk getting caught just to get him a note?

Jared ignored the thought and jotted down what he

wanted to say. He prayed that Shawn would hang around after the hunters walked ahead, and if he knew his best friend, he would do just that. They understood not to talk out loud to one another. But a note . . . that might just work. He was careful with what he wrote and when he felt he was done, he folded up the piece of paper and lifted the door just enough to provide a crack of light. He focused on the bushes where Shawn had been, but they were empty. Did Shawn really leave? The voices were gone. Jared didn't dare abandon the safety of the Dude Cave yet. He slid the note out just enough so it would be visible to anyone who knew where to look, then he brought the door back down, letting the weight of it keep the paper from blowing away in the breeze.

And then he waited. Time inched along, dragging so slowly that Jared started nodding off. His body had exerted so much energy in such a short amount of time that every limb, every muscle ached as if he'd run back-to-back marathons. His head dropped forward, succumbing to the exhaustion . . .

. . . then he jolted awake when something moved outside. He zoned in on the paper, hoping that if someone grabbed it, it was Shawn and not some hunter who would have him trapped like a rat in a cage. Jared was ready to give up when the paper moved, shrinking a few inches as something pulled on it, then disappeared entirely.

Please be Shawn . . .

He waited. Jared closed his eyes and prayed. He prayed to a God he didn't even believe in, desperate for any form of help. A knock. Jared's breath stopped. His fingers dug into the dirt, heart slamming against his ribs.

Another knock. Then—

Rap-tap-tap.

The rhythm sent a shiver through him. He knew that pattern. Morse code.

Shawn. He got the message.

If this paid off, it could not only help Jared survive the night, it could be the start of the town getting rid of the curse. For once, Jared had hope. He didn't just want to survive the curse; he wanted to end it.

PART EIGHT
THE DEAD ZONE

Jared stared at the ceiling of the Dude Cave, debating. He was safe. He had food. He could wait. But that note . . . Shawn was now in danger. He knew leaving was stupid. But not leaving? That felt worse. His biggest concern wasn't navigating through the forest—although that was high on the list—but the fear that he would brave the dangers of making it to the dead zone only to discover it wasn't real. A second concern was that other hunters in town knew about the dead zones and planted hunters at each location. Though that seemed unlikely, as there was no way he wouldn't have heard of such a thing had it been common knowledge.

But what about Wes Tremblay? He clearly knows about them, and he enjoys hunting.

Jared looked over the map again, counting the number of dead zones. There were five of them, all spread out in different parts of town. Three of them were deep in the woods, but the remaining two were actually in town, with one located right around the perimeter of the town hall. That had to have been what Ms. Hendrix was referring to. How was that even possible? That the place the largest groups gathered, was also one of the safe spaces? And how were the dead zones even established? Were they planted by the "creators" of Mail Day? Or a glitch in the system?

Once he thought enough time had passed, Jared propped the door open high enough so he could climb out, then packed his bag with some more supplies, including the bear spray in case he crossed paths with any dogs. He was careful to avoid getting more of it on his hand, and just the thought of it touching his skin again ignited a phantom burning sensation. He cursed at himself under his breath, pissed off that he was so careless with it before. To be safe, he wrapped the can in his wet shirt, then stuffed it in the bag with the rest of his supplies. With one last scan along the perimeter, Jared climbed out of the hole and got to his feet. He immediately looked in the direction Shawn had taken off, finding the coast clear.

This is stupid. You were safe. You had food. Why are you risking everything to try and find a dead zone?

Because, if it's true, this is bigger than surviving a few hours in peace and quiet. It could be the start of finding a way to end this whole thing.

Jared took off toward his destination, holding the map as he went. According to the withered paper, he shouldn't have to travel more than a few miles before reaching the first dead zone. How he'd know what he was looking for was another question, as there was only a small symbol on the map next to each *DZ*. The odds of these spaces being marked were slim, as that would raise concerns in town. And how would Shawn find the exact spot without the map? He was always the better of the two with directions when they traveled out in the woods, but that didn't mean he'd know exactly where to go.

Up ahead, Jared spotted something out of the ordinary in the mix of trees and bushes. At first, he thought it was a person hiding behind a tall pine, waiting for him to approach. But then, as he inched closer, Jared realized it wasn't a person at all but a shirt, hanging from a branch. Not just any shirt; it was Shawn's hoodie. They had come this way. Was he attempting to warn Jared? Did something happen to Shawn?

Jared crouched and took careful strides to avoid stepping on any dead branches. He observed the surrounding space, looking for any sign of Shawn or whoever was out hunting with his best friend. When he felt he was alone, he made his way to the shirt, afraid to grab it at first. Something didn't feel right. He circled the hanging branch, careful not to touch anything. All the uncertainty had Jared wanting to turn back and run for the Dude Cave. Just say, "Fuck it," and take his chances in the hole. It was something he strongly considered until he saw the note he had written Shawn poking out of the shirt pocket.

He grabbed the paper, scanning for any differences. The front of the page appeared unchanged. Jared flipped the paper over.

New handwriting. Not Shawn's.

His stomach clenched.

MEET AT THE DEAD ZONE OR YOUR FRIEND DIES.

The words felt too calm.

Jared's pulse slammed in his ears. Hiding wasn't an option anymore.

He considered sprinting through the forest until he found

the dead zone, but he thought better of it. If he was going to save his best friend, he would have to be smarter than that.

Think! Think of every scenario!

Whoever was out hunting with Shawn must not have known about Jared at the Dude Cave. Otherwise, they would have just ended things right then and there. They must have discovered the note in Shawn's possession while they were walking, maybe even right here where the shirt was hanging. But if that was the case, why not just wait here for him? Hide in the trees and wait for him to discover the note.

A *snap* from the surrounding woods jolted his attention toward the trees. He didn't spot anyone, but he could *feel* them. Someone or something was watching him. Jared froze, as if remaining still would help hide him even though he was out in the open. The breeze continued swaying the branches, making it nearly impossible to determine whether it was the wind moving them or a hunter closing in.

He didn't have time to think about it. Jared took off in a sprint toward the dead zone—at least, in the direction where he knew it was located. He half expected someone to yell behind him, warning the others that he'd been found. But there were no shouts, only his own heavy breathing. He kept running, and running, and running. He ran deep into the forest until his legs refused to do it anymore. Until his lungs burned so intensely that he felt like clawing through his own chest to relieve the pain.

Just when he wanted to give up, to sit down and curl into a ball until someone discovered him and ended things, he spotted a landmark that was clearly out of place. A symbol carved into a towering maple tree, the bark worn with age, but the symbol was painted a bright white as if a fresh layer had been applied. He pulled the map back out of his pocket and located the dead zone. It was the same symbol.

"Holy shit!"

Excitement quickly changed to panic as he realized that, yes, he found the dead zone and it was a real thing, but that also meant Shawn and the hunter were nearby somewhere. It meant that Shawn was in danger, and so was Jared. So, where were they? Did Jared beat them here? Was that them he'd heard before he took off?

"Looking like a deer in headlights, boy."

Jared spun.

Wes Tremblay stood there, grinning like a wolf.

And he wasn't alone.

He had Shawn by the collar, dragging him like a dog on a leash.

It wasn't an old lady with Shawn after all, but Tremblay with his higher Southern drawl that was masked by a set of smoker's lungs.

"Just run, Jared. Don't worry about me!" Shawn yelled, but he was cut short as Wes backhanded him across the face, sending him to the ground.

"Shut up, you little shit. You're lucky I don't have you killed for trying to aid a recipient," Wes said, then turned his attention back to Jared. "I see you found my map, huh? I wondered where I left that thing all these years. Figured someone would find it eventually."

"Please, let Shawn go. He didn't try to help me. I left him a note, not the other way around."

"I'm no fool, kid. I know you two are in cahoots. Why you think I requested to hunt with him? But yeah, these places are real. Which means we aren't being listened to right now. And I can get rid of both of you if I decide to without needing to explain myself."

"Listened to by who?"

"None of your damn business is *who*. All that matters is that this train doesn't go off the rails. You get me, kid? I'm not about to let you ruin it for the whole town."

Jared felt his throat tighten up, the panic kicking into high gear, but he had to play it cool. Maybe if he got Wes to talk, at least Shawn could live to retain some of that information for future generations. It didn't make any damn sense that Wes knew so much about Mail Day, yet he kept it to himself as if that somehow benefited the town. What would benefit the town more was knowing the weaknesses of what created this.

"I don't understand. Why do you still do this? You made it. You're safe. Do you actually enjoy killing people?"

Shawn moaned on the ground, rubbing his face where he'd been struck. Wes kicked him in the stomach, sending Shawn rolling over onto his back, crying in pain.

"Stay down, shithead," Wes snarled, turning back to Jared. "Yeah . . . as a matter of fact, I *do*. But this ain't about me. It's about this town and keeping it in order. I let you walk or let your friend help you, and that order gets one step closer to falling apart. You done me a favor finding that map because now I won't have to worry about anyone else finding it ever again."

"Why not try to end this thing? Instead of going through this crap every year. You've survived this. You could help end it," Jared said.

Wes laughed and shook his head.

"Kid, you really are that ignorant, huh? *They* could kill us all with the snap of their fingers if they so choose. You've seen the pictures. And after the bullshit at the junkyard earlier, you saw how quickly things changed. I'm selfish, sure. But I know that the first ounce of hope those people in town get, this could all come crumbling down, and I ain't risking something I worked hard to survive just to get killed with the rest of 'em."

Jared thought back to that smoke monster. It seemed as though it had formed from the factory's silo and was sent to avenge the rules Mr. Kaine had broken. He tried to stare up through the trees at the sky, hoping maybe the monster would come back and take care of Wes Tremblay. If only he could be that lucky. As scary as the smoke-thing was, there were still so many things that didn't make any sense to Jared.

"So, if you don't break any rules, how'd you know this was really a dead zone? How could you have tested it if you weren't talking to someone about it before? Nobody can survive this night on their own. I'm sure of it. You and Ms. Hendrix must have had someone helping you. And I know whoever it was, they talked to you in one of these places."

"Yeah, kid. I talked to someone. And I bet that old hag Hendrix did too. Nobody survives alone. Nobody. That's why I watched your friend after the mayor questioned him. Knew if anyone was dumb enough to help a runner . . . it'd be him. So, yeah. That's how I found out the dead zones were more than just a rumor. And that's why I've killed more people in past years who tried to use them. It's nothing personal, kid. Now, enough chitchatting, get over here and let's get this over with."

Jared didn't move. Not because he was intentionally disobedient but because he was too scared. His brain was spinning, trying to think of any possible way out of this scenario. And then he noticed Shawn slowly getting to his feet behind Wes. Somehow, he'd crawled away while Wes was distracted talking. Jared needed to keep him talking longer.

"Fine . . . but since you're killing me anyway, you might as well tell me. Ms. Hendrix hinted at checking out the town hall when I talked with her before Mail Day. Made it sound like it was a safe place or something. What was she talking about?"

"That gabby bitch. Eh, fuck it, you're dying anyway. There's tunnels. Start at a hidden door in the town hall and travel beneath Pembroke. Nobody's supposed to find them. There's stuff down there that's never meant to be seen. But I know that's how she survived. She found the tunnels and the rest of the town had no idea where to look for her. How she discovered them, I'd like to know. But I plan on keeping their location secret. Now that I know she's been feeding information to you, I think I might just have to pay that wrinkled bitch a visit."

Fireworks of realization exploded in Jared's head. It all made so much sense now, yet somehow the town had been blinded from the truth. And it explained why Ms. Hendrix was willing to risk saying something to him in the town hall —it was one of the dead zones. Sure, she still had to worry about others hearing her, but she didn't need to worry about *Them*. Jared also realized that Wes had every intention of harming or even killing the poor old woman, when all she wanted to do was help others survive.

Shawn continued climbing to his feet behind Wes, who was stepping toward Jared, unaware that Shawn was now standing. Jared spotted a gun at Wes's side and hoped Shawn did something before the hunter pulled it.

"So, what's the point of these tunnels? What's down there that you say nobody is supposed to see?" Jared asked, hoping the tremble in his voice didn't give away his attempt at distraction.

"I'm done telling you shit, kid. You see that symbol on the tree? That's all part of this. It's much bigger than anything this pissant town can comprehend. And only certain people understand that. Now get the fuck over here and stop dragging this out."

Wes went for his gun, but Shawn launched himself onto Wes's back, wrapping his arm around the hunter's throat and squeezing. The initial shock didn't last long, though, and the muscular frame of Wes Tremblay was too much for a scrawny teenage boy to handle. Wes flipped Shawn over his shoulder, sending him sailing to the ground, his back impacting the forest floor with a solid *thud*. Shawn gasped for breath—the wind completely knocked out of him. Jared took advantage of the distraction, charging at Wes, attempting to take him out at the knees. Wes's one knee buckled, but he didn't go down. Instead, he grabbed Jared by the collar and threw him to the ground next to Shawn. Jared's bag slid across the bumpy terrain, sending all the contents scattering across the dead foliage.

"I'm going to have to get rid of both you obnoxious little shits. Now, this *is* personal," Wes snarled.

Again, he went for the gun, but Shawn crawled forward, trying to stop him from getting hold of the firearm. Wes kicked Shawn in the mouth, sending a few chipped teeth into the air, a trail of blood not far behind. As he grabbed the gun from its holster, Jared crawled over to his bag and found the bear spray. He wasn't worried about burning his hand this time. Instead, he gripped it tightly as Wes aimed the gun at the back of Shawn's head.

"No!" Jared yelled, jumping to his feet with the can in hand.

Wes shifted his attention to Jared, looking just in time to see a stream of spray infiltrate his eyes. The gun went off, a *CRACK* that sent a bullet into a nearby tree as Wes screamed, reaching for his eyes. Jared grabbed a fallen tree limb. He swung it, connecting with Wes Tremblay's open mouth, cutting his screams short. The weapon fell to the ground as Wes stumbled back, tripping over Shawn's foot and landing on his ass.

Jared dropped to his knees and scurried to the gun, which immediately felt foreign in his grip. He was surprised by the weight of it, only having ever played with toy guns with Shawn when they were much younger. It was as though the gun was made of dry ice, sending a tingling sensation all the way up his arm. Wes writhed on the ground, clawing at his eyes.

"You son of a bitch! Fuck!"

Jared tasted the bear spray that had slowly evaporated around him as he inched closer to his attacker. Shawn was still on the ground, in a great deal of pain. It dawned on Jared what he needed to do, and he felt sick to his stomach. He had to shoot Wes Tremblay. He had to kill another living person. After seeing multiple dead bodies for the first time in his life today, Jared had to add to that tally if he wanted to save himself and Shawn from this madman.

He slowly raised the pistol, his arm trembling. Wes had already begun getting to his feet, still trying to blink away the poison coating his pupils.

Wes charged.

Jared didn't think.

His finger squeezed the trigger.

The gun kicked, snapping his wrist. A deafening *CRACK* rang through the trees.

Wes's head jerked back.

A hole bloomed between his left eye and his nose.

For half a second, he stood. Then his knees buckled.

He collapsed. Face-first onto the dirt.

Jared dropped the gun, his breath ragged, his stomach twisting.

He had just killed a man.

Blood immediately pooled under Wes's head, but the puddle was the only thing moving. Wes Tremblay was dead. Jared dropped to his knees, and the tears came full force. He cried until he heard Shawn moaning, trying to get to his feet but struggling to even lift his head.

"Shawn!"

He ran to his best friend, helping him sit up, gasping at the instant black eye and busted mouth that he now presented.

"It's that bad, huh?" Shawn asked.

Even in a time of distress, he still found a way to make Jared smile. The smile was short-lived as he noticed Shawn staring at the corpse.

Shawn wiped blood from his mouth, never taking his eyes off Wes's body.

His voice was hoarse. "You had to, man. He was gonna kill us. And Hendrix."

"I know. I— We need to get out of here. They'll come toward the direction of the gunshots. We have to find a place to get out of sight."

"The town hall. We need to get to those tunnels, right?"

Jared considered their options. As soon as the boys left the dead zone, would they run the risk of the hunters discovering he and Shawn were working together? They had no choice but to risk it, though. He wasn't about to leave Shawn for dead. The thought of heading back toward town, leaving the cover of the forest, and going out into the open terrified him.

"Yeah. Do you think you can make it there?"

Shawn laughed, forcing some blood spatter to spray from his mouth.

"If this doesn't work, we're dead anyway. Even if it does work, we still might be. When Mayor Thompson finds out we not only helped each other but killed a non-recipient, we're done for. They'll make an accident happen with each of our families. So . . . yeah, I think I can make it. Because we have no other options."

"We have to go before they find us," Jared said, numbly staring at the dead body of Wes Tremblay as he made out with the dirt. The shock likely wouldn't go away anytime soon, and he dreaded the day it would.

Shawn walked up to Wes and at first, Jared thought he was going to kick the dead man. Instead, he slid piles of leaves over the body, repeating the process until the corpse was mostly covered. It reminded Jared of when they'd hidden their bikes so nobody would discover them heading out to the Dude Cave. As ridiculous as it was, Jared couldn't help but feel a bit of disappointment knowing their secret hideout would likely never be used again. That emotion was replaced with his recollection that it did save his life, so for that, he was thankful.

After packing up his spilled belongings into his backpack, Jared tucked the gun in the outside pouch, keeping it separate from his other supplies. He grabbed the map, happy to see that it was mostly unharmed in the struggle, then looked straight at the path ahead.

"Okay . . . let's do this."

PART NINE
THE TOWN HALL

The boys finally reached the end of the forest at the edge of town. Jared's thoughts were a scattered mess.

At any moment, the thing in the sky could return.

At any moment, someone could spot them.

One wrong move, and it wouldn't just be him dead. Shawn. His family. They would all pay for what he had done. Pembroke didn't mess around when it came to the rules of Mail Day. And they had now broken the *biggest* rules of the event.

The belief was that as long as you didn't talk, *They* couldn't track you. But Jared had no proof of that. Just like he and Shawn had no evidence that dead zones actually existed until a few hours ago. If there was any silver lining in all of this, it was that it was now midday, and the last few hours had flown by.

"Okay, looks like this takes us out just on the other side of the junkyard. That's where Maxine got whacked by her dad last year," Shawn said.

Jared didn't find the comment amusing, picturing what his own father would do in that situation. He knew it was extremely likely his parents would find him. They knew their kid. And unlike Shawn, they followed the rules. If there was one thing his mom and dad cared about as much as their son, it was immunity. He just hoped they didn't cross paths until the next morning.

"We have to be careful here, man. There's no telling if they're still cleaning up the mess of Maxine's dad and the others in there. And we have to stop talking—at least until we reach the next dead zone," Jared said, hoping that even those words weren't enough to trigger something from *Them.*

If they made it to the town hall, then they could find a place to set up camp and talk. Come up with a plan.

Come up with a plan. That's all I keep trying to do and failing miserably at it.

It's not like there's a playbook to this. If there was, we'd have more than two survivors.

One survivor. I just killed the other.

Jared hadn't let himself process it yet.

He killed a man.

Shot him. Watched the life drain from his eyes as his body staggered and dropped. Covered his body in dead leaves like he was nothing but litter.

If he survived this, would he ever be able to sleep again? Would Wes's face be waiting for him in the dark?

And then hiding that secret from his family? He couldn't admit to it because that would defeat the entire purpose of trying to survive Mail Day. The thought of making it, surviving through the night only to be cuffed and made to serve life for murder, made him nauseous. Being on the run, constantly looking over his shoulder for hunters, kept his mind off what he did. But he knew that any time he closed his eyes, he'd see the image of Wes Tremblay bleeding out of the bullet wound in his face.

The junkyard was empty of any hunters, so they stepped out, crouching low and remaining hidden behind the recycling containers. To reach the town hall, they would have to travel through a good portion of town without much cover. It felt like a death trap, but so did every other place Jared had tried to spend any amount of time. The town hall, specifically what was *beneath* the town hall, was more than just a chance at survival. It was hope. Hope that this curse could be erased forever, giving Pembroke residents a chance to move on. No longer scared to open their mailboxes. No more dreading the one day of the year that turned the entire town into a pack of murderers.

Jared needed to communicate with Shawn. An idea came to him, and he knelt behind the metal container and unzipped his bag. Shawn motioned as if to say, "What the hell are you doing?" but Jared ignored him, pulling out the notebook. He wrote quickly, the handwriting messy and borderline illegible. When he was done, he handed the notebook to Shawn so he could read the message.

If we cut through the alleyways between the businesses in town, we might be able to avoid any hunters. There's always a chance they have someone waiting in those places, but it's a safer bet than walking out in the open. What do you think?

Shawn read it and shrugged, but the look on his face indicated that he wasn't convinced. He took the pen from Jared and wrote something, then handed back the notebook.

Ok. This sucks, but I don't have a better plan.

Also, your handwriting is dogshit.

Jared looked up. Shawn smirked. Jared flipped him off.

And with that, they were on their way again, trying to avoid what felt like an inevitable death.

***

By the time they reached the center of town, the sun had already begun its descent behind the trees. As luck would have it, they arrived as most families entered their homes for dinner. While there would always be teams out hunting, this happened to be the time of day with the least amount of traffic. After dinner, though, would be another story. The intensity amped up, the dogs unleashed. Police and volunteers would slowly drive up and down every single street until first light the next morning when the hunt ended. For any recipients fortunate to last that long, it evoked the "Witching Hour." In other words, all bets were off. Jared knew they had to get to the tunnel before that happened.

The town hall was visible from the alleyway behind Al's Diner where they currently hid, yet it felt so far away. Making it this far had been a miracle. None of that would matter if they were discovered before they got inside. Every single move mattered. Every breath. Every step. Jared couldn't help but feel that there were invisible land mines scattered every few feet, and one wrong move would be the end. He looked down at Shawn, who was crouched behind a dumpster. Jared pressed himself against the wall, ready to look out and determine if they could make a run to the next narrow space between buildings. The scent of expired food wafted from the dumpster, and it took all Jared could do to stop himself from gagging. If he could speak, the moment would have been a perfect opportunity to rib Shawn about how the scent of rotten fish smelled like his mom.

A bell jingled as the diner door opened, and Jared dropped back down by Shawn, gesturing to be quiet. Footsteps increased in volume, getting closer. The diner wasn't even open on Mail Day, so why the hell was someone leaving? This couldn't be the way things ended— getting killed next to a dumpster full of rotten fish. The footsteps stopped right around the corner of the building. Had someone seen them coming into the alley?

"Hey, it's Thompson."

Jared's heart launched into his throat. Was the mayor talking to them?

". . . . . . Yeah. Where are you at?" the mayor asked. Again, Jared thought he must be talking to them, but then he spoke once more, and it was clear he was on the phone. The flicker of a lighter, then the smell of a cigarette combined with the dead fish to create a nauseating blend. ". . . . . . I'm about to head down to my office and talk with *Them*. They're not pleased with how this year's shaking out. Fucking Kaine, that psychopath . . . . . . Yeah. He put this entire town in danger. We should've been keeping a closer eye on him after last year."

Jared and Shawn looked at one another, and their expressions said it all. The mayor was on the phone, and he was talking about whoever was responsible for Mail Day. He played it off in the town meetings like he didn't know who *They* were. And it wasn't just the mayor that apparently knew. Who was on the other end of that phone call?

All the boys could do at this point was wait and hope the mayor didn't take a few more steps in their direction. Dread forced itself down Jared's throat, creating an icy ball of fear in the pit of his stomach. *Please, not like this. If I'm going to die, at least let me try to end this curse first.*

". . . . . . Wes isn't answering. Last I heard, he was tracking the boy near the junkyard. But then Kaine—"

A frustrated exhale.

"That psychopath screwed us. The Witching Hour is our last shot. There's no way the kid survives past then. You have to trust me—"

Mayor Thompson coughed, breaking up his sentence. At first, Jared thought he had just inhaled too much of his cigarette, but then the mayor gagged.

"Christ on a stick! Al needs to empty this goddamn dumpster. Smells like death out here."

Another step in their direction.

". . . . . . Yeah, I'm heading down now. Keep me posted on the kid."

The call ended, and the mayor continued muttering something under his breath about the stench as he walked away. Jared let out the breath he'd been holding, a sudden burning sensation releasing from the center of his chest. The mayor was gone, but that was only part of the problem. His office was in the town hall. Did it really make sense to go there when they knew he would be in the building?

Jared tried to remember where the mayor's office was located and recalled it being off to the left of the stage where he gave his big Mail Day speeches every year. They would just need to avoid getting too close to that space. Jared approached the corner, ready to look out again, when Shawn squeezed his arm and pulled him back down.

"What the hell are you doing?" Shawn mouthed silently.

"We need to go, before the Witching Hour," Jared mouthed back.

Shawn sighed, but he knew Jared was right. Both boys peered out, discovering an empty street. For the next twenty minutes, they carefully moved from one alley to the next, checking all possible exits, listening for any sounds, then repeating the process. Finally, they reached the town hall. Relieved, it took everything in Jared to stop himself from bursting through the front door.

Shawn motioned around the side of the building, and Jared followed. Even being extra cautious, he couldn't help but feel as if eyes were burning into his back, watching his every move. Of course, he knew it couldn't possibly be true because if anyone spotted him, they wouldn't waste their time sneaking up for the right moment. Nobody would be dumb enough to risk losing a shot at immunity. Along the side of the town hall, a wooden fence wrapped around the perimeter to block them from the main road.

When they made it to the rear of the building, Shawn pointed at the back door, gesturing first for Jared to pull the map back out. He grabbed it from the bag and quickly scanned it, and if the markings were correct, they had reached the dead zone. Before he felt comfortable talking, he thought back to the dead zone in the woods and the symbol that matched the one on the map. Would there be a similar design here somewhere?

He inspected the old wood siding, sliding his fingers along the surface in case the symbol had been painted over in the years since it had been carved. Jared wouldn't risk speaking until he knew for sure. Shawn blocked him and put his hands up in confusion.

"Look for this symbol somewhere close by. I found one at the last dead zone," Jared mouthed, making sure to exaggerate each word.

With that, they spread out, letting the privacy of the fence allow them to let their guard down. Jared kept reminding himself not to do it. Never assume you're safe, his dad had warned at breakfast. As he continued to search, Shawn snapped his fingers from the other corner of the building. Jared ran to him and felt a jolt of excitement when he stared down at the large rock that Shawn had lifted, revealing the symbol on the bottom. Jared took a deep breath and let out some of the stress that had built up.

"Okay, we know we're in the dead zone now. But we still have to be careful how loud we talk. And we have to remember that Wes Tremblay knew of the dead zones, so others might as well. Especially Mayor Thompson," Jared whispered.

"Let's check the back door. The stairs to the basement are on this side of the building. You have to figure that any secret door leading underground would be there, right?"

"Yeah . . . unless it's less obvious than that. What if there's a secret door on the first floor somewhere that bypasses the basement?"

"You watch too many spy movies. They left the symbol on a fucking rock, man. How sophisticated do you think they are? They just use the town's fear against us, expecting us to go along with it all and not go digging for answers."

Jared hoped that was true, but his gut still told him that whoever was in charge wasn't as stupid as Shawn made them out to be. He thought they wanted the dead zones to be accessible to the recipients of the envelope, like creating checkpoints similar to video games he played. This was all part of their sick game. And he was going to get to the bottom of why they were doing it.

He slowly turned the handle and pushed the door open, wincing as the old, rusted hinges squealed. He froze, listening to see if the noise brought any attention, and when nobody came, he entered the town hall with Shawn right behind him. The back of the building smelled of mothballs and cheap air fresheners, but it sure as hell beat the smell of the dumpster at Al's. Once they were all the way in, the silence was disturbingly infinite. Every other time Jared had been inside the town hall, there were meetings or gatherings, and the murmuring of the crowd was engrained as part of the town hall's identity. Now, it was dark and silent, as if the building had been deserted long ago. A place that looked so familiar now felt so foreign.

"There, that door should go to the basement," Shawn whispered, pointing down the hall.

As they approached it, a light snapped on in the meeting room at the end of the corridor. The mayor walked across their field of vision, from one end of the main room to the other, thankfully without noticing them standing there. Jared didn't dare go for the basement door with it still five feet away. They couldn't risk Thompson coming back across the room and spotting them. Instead, Jared opened the closet on the opposite wall. He pulled Shawn in and gently shut the door, leaving it open just a few inches to see out.

"He'll see us in here," Shawn whispered.

"Maybe . . . but we know for sure he would have seen us if we tried to make it to the basement door. We wait in here until the coast is clear again."

The closet wasn't big enough for one person to stand in comfortably, let alone two. But they made it work, cramming together with a sliver of light bleeding in from the hall. After another moment of silence, Mayor Thompson spoke, "Listen . . . I'm doing everything I can to keep this in order. You know we don't have these issues any other year. I'm not sure what the hell's going on this year, but I'll clean it up."

Jared assumed he was on the phone again, but then another voice spoke, low and almost demonic sounding. Just the hum of it sent gooseflesh across Jared's arms.

"You know the consequences. Do you have eyes on the kid right now?"

"N-no. But I'm working on it. I'm waiting to hear back from Tremblay, who followed a lead out in the woods behind the junkyard. Soon it'll be the Witching Hour and there's no chance of him escaping when that happens. You need to trust me."

"*Trust.* If we trusted you, we wouldn't need to watch over you. Witching Hour is supposed to be a backup plan, not something you people depend on every year. This is two years in a row now."

"I'm sorry. I know we've slipped up in the last few years. But we haven't had a survivor in almost twenty years, and before that, it was another forty years. We have a high success rate. And I know how much the sacrifice means to you. We—"

"Enough! I'm sick of listening to excuses. If the sacrifice is not complete by dawn, you will suffer greatly."

"Please . . . Pembroke is under so much pressure. Everyone is trying their hardest. His parents are answering all the questions we ask. Don't make the town suffer."

"I said *you* will suffer. You are a pawn in this game that can easily be replaced. Nightfall is upon us. You better not fail, scum." The voice deepened, vibrating the walls.

"We won't—" the mayor started, but then a loud *bang*, like a table breaking, cut him off.

"Words are useless. Get it done."

Footsteps approached the hall, and Jared regretted not shutting the closet door all the way. Whoever this was, he was dangerous. If they spotted Jared, especially with an ally helping him, things would get ugly fast.

A shadow stretched along the opposite wall.

Jared pressed into the darkness, his shoulder digging into Shawn.

The air in the closet turned thick.

The figure outside stopped moving.

And then—

A slow, wet inhale.

Jared's heart rate accelerated like a beating drum, and then the figure appeared. He was too tall.

Unnaturally stretched. Lanky.

His skin was the color of pale gray candle wax, his cheeks so hollowed they looked carved.

And his eyes.

Black voids with tiny, burning red pinpricks in the center.

Jared's stomach churned. This thing wasn't human.

Over his white dress shirt that was closer to a shade of yellow, he wore suspenders which held up his loose trousers.

Jared covered his mouth. He considered closing his eyes. As if not seeing this man would somehow make the man not see him. *Don't move. Don't move. Blend in with the darkness.*

While the man *appeared* human, just being in his presence filled Jared with a sense of dread he had never felt before. More so than even opening the red envelope with his name on it.

Why did he stop right out there? Did he see us?

His long nose twitched.

He took a slow, dragging inhale—like a wolf testing the air for blood.

Please keep going . . . Please.

"Thompson!" the tall man snapped, revealing teeth that had browned along the edges.

"Y-yes? What is it?"

"The boy is near . . . I can smell him. Get your people up this way and do it now."

The snarl on the man's face almost made Jared release his bladder, but he forced himself to hold it in. If this thing could smell him now, his piss would be a dead giveaway.

"Yes, sir. I'm on it," the mayor said, then his steps left the area, proceeding deeper into the town hall.

The tall man huffed, then continued walking, storming through the back door.

Jared wanted to take a deep breath, but he didn't dare yet. He waited until the pain in his chest was unbearable, then let it out, allowing the relief to finally set in that they hadn't been discovered. Yet.

"What . . . the . . . fuck was that?" Shawn whispered.

"I don't know. We need to get to the basement, now. Let's go," Jared said.

Slowly, Shawn pushed the door open, half expecting the tall man to be on the other side waiting for him, but the hall was empty. He motioned Jared out, and they hurried down the hall until they reached the basement door. Thankfully, it was unlocked. Jared didn't even realize he was crying until a tear slid down his cheek, which he quickly wiped away. The stairs heading to the basement were dark and musty, but there was no way he dared turn the light on. The boys shut the door quietly behind them, then began their descent.

Jared and Shawn braved the dark.

The Tall Man's red pupils burned in their minds.

Watching.

Waiting.

PART TEN
DARKNESS, TAKE MY HAND

"Man, who the hell was that guy? He didn't look human," Shawn whispered as the boys moved slowly down the dark stairs.

"More like, *what* was that guy? I don't have a clue, but it's obvious Mayor Thompson knows more than he tells the town. Whoever that freak is . . . he's part of the bigger picture. Didn't his face look kind of familiar to you?"

"No, man. Never seen that creepy bastard in my life," Shawn said, then almost stumbled down one of the stairs. "Hey, didn't you bring a flashlight or something?"

Jared stopped on the second to last stair to grab his bag, and Shawn walked into his back. The basement was pitch-black, and their eyes hadn't adjusted at all yet.

"Watch it, dude. You want the light or not? I didn't want to use it until we got far enough from the door," Jared whispered.

"Next time warn me if you're going to stop in the dark

like that," Shawn said, then Jared heard his friend sniffing the air. "Smells like ass down here. Like your old gym clothes or something."

"More like your mom's underwear," Jared said.

"Always with the mom jokes . . . Screw you. "

Finally, Jared's fingers closed around the flashlight. He clicked it on, and the cone sliced through the swallowing dark, revealing the guts of the town hall's basement.

Thick cobwebs hung from wooden beams. Stacks of dusty town records leaned at dangerous angles, ready to topple.

And something reeked.

Not just old wood and mold. Something deeper. Wetter.

Like something had rotted.

"Jesus, when's the last time anyone came down here? Looks straight out of a haunted house movie," Jared said.

He stepped down onto the floor and scanned the room with the light, finding it mostly just full of storage items from the town—shelves full of books and files that looked like they hadn't been touched in years. He walked slowly, with Shawn at his side, stopping every few feet to look for any signs of a secret door. Instead, all he discovered were stacks of cardboard boxes, likely full of more useless town history.

Jared stared at the leaning stacks of records.

Mail Day.

What if the truth was here? Buried under years of dust and silence?

His fingers twitched.

He wanted to tear open every box. He wanted to rip through the town's secrets.

But not yet. Not yet.

It was just as likely that Mayor Thompson was a chronic hoarder. There wasn't time to open every single box. They were on a mission, and Jared had no intention of straying from that again. They moved farther into the darkness, momentarily freezing when they heard footsteps thumping overhead. Then came the mayor's muffled voice again. They couldn't make out the words, but it was enough for Jared to realize that they had to be conscious of how loud they were. If the boys could hear things up there, that meant the mayor might hear them if they weren't careful.

When the footsteps moved away from them, they continued searching. Next up, Jared came to a pile of old Mail Day decorations—signs, banners, and even a large mural that one of the residents had painted for the town. In years past, Pembroke used to decorate the day after to celebrate making it through another year. Those celebrations stopped the year a high school boy named Nicholas Hall charged into the town hall with a gun, threatening to shoot everyone he'd witnessed hunting for his sister on Mail Day. It was an ugly scene, and Nicholas had to be apprehended. Word spread that they'd sent him away to the nut house. Jared wasn't sure how true that was, but he hadn't seen the kid since.

"Maybe if you survive the night, you can wave the banner proud tomorrow like a big old flag," Shawn said.

"Real funny. Glad to see you joking about me dying."

"Hey, I'm joking about you *living*. There's a difference."

"Let's hold off on talking until we know for sure we're far enough away to avoid being heard," Jared said.

The boys spent the better part of an hour searching the entire basement for some mystical door that didn't appear to be there. Jared gritted his teeth, ready to just give up and hide out in the basement for as long as they could. They knew it was a dead zone, so at least they had that going for them. Plus, he had snacks in his bag. Maybe he was getting in too deep trying to play the hero. He was just a kid. Why not save the knight in shining armor role for someone older who didn't have a whole life ahead of them?

No, I've known from the beginning that if I ever got picked, I wouldn't just hide and wait. I would try to save the whole town because I want a normal life that I've never been able to live.

While the thought was true, it was a lot easier to think it than actually *do* it. Just like when he was hiding in the Dude Cave, he had found a great spot to, at the very least, knock a few hours off the hunt. Who knew? Maybe Ms. Hendrix only meant to come down here to hide. Maybe she never found the tunnels and only Wes Tremblay had. Jared sat on the floor and leaned back against the concrete wall, frustrated with the lack of discovery. This really felt like it was going to be big, and yet they were no better off than before. He set the flashlight down next to him and let the beam of light point up at the ceiling like a makeshift lantern. He needed to think. Obviously, the tunnels wouldn't be easy to find. If they were, others would have discovered them years ago. Maybe there really was a hidden door somewhere else in the town hall that led to the tunnels.

"We aren't going about this the right way, man. The door wouldn't just be out in the open. It's hidden. We need to move stuff, look for anything out of place," Jared whispered.

"Dude . . . we've literally checked this place from top to bottom. I could name every object stored down here at this point. We need to face the fact that it's not down here. I was wrong, you happy?" Shawn asked.

"No. I'd rather you be right for once than waste so much time searching for something that doesn't exist. This is pointless."

"What if Wes was lying? Yeah, he thought he was going to kill us, so revealing his little secret wouldn't matter, but why would he have even wanted to let his guard down and spill that information?"

Jared shook his head. He didn't want to believe that. *Couldn't* believe that. Because if this was all for nothing . . .

"We keep looking. If you don't want to, that's up to you. But I got nothing better to do. At least it keeps my mind off the time slowly ticking by," Jared said.

"You're such a pain in the ass. We've checked the whole floor. We've looked beneath everything. What do you plan to move that we haven't already? Just give it a rest and pass me a damn energy bar."

Jared jumped to his feet.

"You're a genius! Yes, we've checked the whole floor. And obviously the door wouldn't be on the ceiling. But there are four walls in here, man. Let's go. If you're a good dog, I'll give you your treat after."

"If I was a dog, I'd bite your face off right now."

Jared spotted a smile behind those words as the beam of light displayed Shawn's facial features. He bent down and grabbed the flashlight, then aimed it at the far wall. He carefully slid his fingers along the concrete, feeling for any difference in the surface. This had to be it. The first wall brought nothing but more doubt. As Jared moved to the second wall, he held the light parallel with the concrete and noticed a slight curve in the center. To the unsuspecting eye, it could be easily missed. It could also simply just be an old building starting to shift, which was a normal occurrence in New Hampshire after so many cold winters.

Still, it gave him hope, something running in short supply

these days. Shawn stared at Jared, who had his head close to the wall and his empty hand rubbing the concrete.

"Why don't you make out with it? Want me to go somewhere else so you can confess your love?"

"Shut up. I liked it better when you were hurt. I see something on this wall; it's curved in the middle."

Shawn walked to the center and pressed on it. There was a crack that traveled along the concrete, and if one looked quick, they would mistake it for an ancient foundation showing its age.

"Well holy shit. This section is separated. Come here," Shawn said.

Jared and Shawn pressed their hands against the wall.

At first, nothing.

Then—

A faint, gritty scrape.

Jared's pulse slammed in his ears.

They pushed again, harder.

The wall shuddered, groaning like an ancient stone door.

And then—

It slid open.

A black maw gaped before them.

And from inside, a cold breath leaked out.

It took everything Jared had not to turn and run the other way. Everything about this space reeked of evil, like a tomb in the center of town.

Jared pointed the flashlight, revealing a narrow passageway between two walls. The floor was covered in mouse droppings and chewed-up newspaper. Old insulation drooped lazily overhead from the ceiling.

"Hope you're not claustrophobic," he whispered, then stepped into the tight space.

In order to fit, Jared realized he had to take his backpack off, turn sideways, and shimmy through pressed up against the wall. He dropped the bag to the floor and slid it using his foot with each step. The opposite wall was less than a foot from his face. There wasn't even enough space to hold his arm up and point the light to make sure there were no random nails sticking out across from him. He pictured sliding through, only to have the head of a tetanus-infested rusty nail scrape along his face.

Stop thinking that. It does no good to get scared by a hypothetical scenario. There are enough real concerns to worry about.

Jared squeezed through, the walls pressing in.

His back scraped against rough concrete. His chest compressed.

He tried to turn his head. His cheek brushed against stone.

The tunnel was getting narrower.

And the air thinner.

Shawn breathed heavily behind him, and he knew his best friend was likely feeling the same anxiety he was. What if they went all the way to the end only to discover it was just a dead end? Or worse, what if a previous recipient of Mail Day had the same idea and didn't make it all the way through, getting stuck where nobody ever discovered them? The last thing Jared's fragile mind could handle right now would be to bump into a corpse that had died years ago and was trapped in here with them.

That reminded Jared that while there were only two survivors to ever make it to the next morning, there was the legend of a recipient that was never found. Jared always thought it was just folklore—a campfire tale created to scare kids of Pembroke. There were many versions of the story. Some ended with the recipient fleeing town while being hunted, which seemed unlikely considering the strict rules in place. Other versions said the recipient found a hiding spot so secluded that they got stuck, died, and nobody ever found them. That couldn't be true, though. If it was, Jared figured it would be discussed more in town meetings. And surely, the mayor would have sent search parties out until they came up with something.

What if the mayor doesn't talk about it because he doesn't want the town to know that it's possible to leave? Or maybe he did send out search parties, only to come up empty-handed.

If that was the case, there would have been a bigger deal made by the residents that a recipient didn't meet one of the two possible outcomes to appease whoever was in charge. You either survived, or you died trying. It was as simple as that. There was no leaving town. No going off the grid and living a peaceful life. If that was possible, others would do it. And if there was a dead body rotting somewhere in Pembroke, wouldn't there be a record of a missing recipient in the town records? Jared had studied the town's history religiously and couldn't recall a skipped year or an asterisk next to any name.

"We almost to the end? I can barely breathe in here," Shawn said.

"I can't tell. It has to be close, though. The building isn't much longer than this."

Sweat dripped down Jared's forehead into his eyes and out of instinct, he tried to lift his free hand to wipe it away, only to crack it on the far wall. The sweat trickled and pooled on his lower eyelids, stinging his pupils.

"There's probably friggin' asbestos down here. This place is old as hell," Shawn complained.

"Asbestos is the least of my worries. I just hope this leads to the tunnels," Jared said, trying to blink the sweat away.

"Look at the bright side. This is killing a ton of time. Plus, there's no way any adult could fit through here, right? It's a great spot to hide, man."

"Wes Tremblay did. I know he was younger when he did it, but I can't imagine he was ever as skinny as us," Jared said.

"Hey . . . You're skinny. I'm jacked."

"Oh, for fuck's sake. It's bad enough I'm stuck between two walls, now I have to listen to you making shit up about those toothpick arms?"

"I'm putting my life on the line to help you, so respect these guns."

Jared laughed and kept moving. Finally, the light revealed the end of the wall. Without even realizing it, he picked up speed, ignoring the rough scraping against his back.

Please . . . this has to be the way.

"We're almost to the end. Cross your fingers," he said.

"I would cross them if I even had enough space to lift them."

A cool draft bled through the wall, chilling the sweat on Jared's face. That had to be a good sign. It meant there was open space on the other side somewhere. He reached the end and he was hit with a moment of panic as it just appeared to be what he dreaded. There was no door or opening, just two walls and a dark corner.

"You've got to be kidding me," Shawn muttered.

"Can't you feel that breeze? Help me push the wall in front of us."

Shawn scoffed but complied. They both pressed their

palms against the concrete and pushed. At first, nothing happened. But then Jared noticed it moved a few inches.

"Keep pushing! It's moving," he said.

He immediately regretted allowing his voice to get so loud, but this was too exciting to care about that right now. They pushed, again moving the section of wall in front of them another foot. The wall was now far enough that they could extend their arms and put more strength behind their efforts. After pushing a few more times, there was enough space to fit in. A sulfuric odor wafted out of the darkness ahead.

Jared covered his nose with his shirt and entered. As he went to take a step in, his foot had nothing to plant on, and he almost fell face-first until Shawn pulled back on his shirt.

"What the—" Jared started, aiming the flashlight toward the floor. Only there was no floor. Instead, they saw an opening that looked more like a giant demonic well ready to suck them up. It was a hole leading deeper underground. *The tunnels.*

"Looks like I just saved your life again, hombre. If we make it out of this, you're giving me all those tasty snacks your mom packs in your lunch for like a year," Shawn said.

He was right. Had he not grabbed hold of him, there was a good chance Jared would have fallen to his death. The light gave off enough illumination that he could see a good twenty feet down, and there was *still* no bottom in sight.

"Thanks, man. I do owe you, for real. But dude . . . we found the tunnels! There's a ladder going down there. Let's see what this is all about."

Jared picked up his backpack and slung it over his shoulder, then stuck the flashlight in his mouth. He crouched to get his foot on the farthest rung he could reach in the hole, taking one step at a time, careful not to lose his footing. Shawn waited until Jared was far enough down, then climbed in himself. It was as if the town hall was testing every single one of Jared's phobias in the span of a few minutes. If there was one thing that he hated more than tight spaces, it was heights.

Knowing my luck, snakes with spider legs will start climbing up the walls from the darkness below.

He shook the ridiculous thought and continued his descent. Each step echoed through the tight space, and Jared couldn't help but think it sounded like a gong clanging. He just hoped it wasn't obvious from above the surface. After about ten feet of climbing, he risked a look down and thought he saw a surface below. When he lifted his head to focus again on the rungs, the end of the flashlight connected with the wall in front of him, the handle cracking against his teeth. Before he could bring up a hand to stop it, the flashlight fell from his mouth, and Jared watched as it spiraled through the air, the beam giving a strobe light show as it spun in circles until it eventually smashed onto the ground below.

"Shit!" Jared yelled.

"Keep it down, genius. At least the light's still working somehow. We can just pick it up when we reach the bottom," Shawn said.

With the light now revealing their destination, Jared guessed they had another fifteen feet to go. The beam aimed off to the side, creating a giant bright spot on the wall but not providing much visibility on the ladder itself. It just made each step that much more dangerous, but Jared wasn't in a rush. He took each rung slowly, keeping his eyes focused below to make sure his footing was stable.

Then—

A scrape.

A shuffling retreating into the dark.

Jared froze.

Not a rat. Too big.

A person?

Or . . .

Something else?

The dark below them was no longer empty.

Shawn almost stepped down on him until he realized Jared wasn't moving.

"What the hell, man? Keep go—"

"*Shhh*! I heard something down there."

He tried to calm his panicked breaths so he could hear better, but the sound didn't come again. When he thought it must be nothing, just his mind playing tricks on him in the dark, he went to take another step down, and a shape ran through the beam of light, disappearing out of sight. This time, he heard its footsteps running until they faded somewhere deeper into the tunnels.

"What the hell was that?" Shawn whispered.

"I-I don't know. Should we go back up?"

"We can't do that, and you know it. We've come way too far to turn back, dude."

Fear planted itself firmly in the pit of Jared's stomach. Shawn was right. They had to keep going. While he didn't get a good look at whatever it was down there, it sure as hell wasn't some small vermin scurrying away in fear. It was big. And while he couldn't be sure, it definitely *appeared* to be the size and shape of a person.

"Whatever it was, it ran off. Now's our chance to get down there," Shawn said.

Jared took a deep breath and climbed the remaining steps

slowly. Eventually he reached the bottom and immediately grabbed the flashlight off the ground, aiming it in the direction the thing ran. There was nothing in front of him but open space. He turned around and checked the opposite direction, seeing only endless darkness.

Shawn reached the last rung and jumped off to land next to Jared.

"This is wild. How the hell did they make this so far beneath the ground? Must have taken years. I don't know about you, but I say we go in the opposite direction of whatever that was," Shawn said.

"Yeah, I agree. Let's go."

The air was cooler down here and gave off an earthy aroma, which was an improvement from the sulfur smell above.

"I can't believe it's real," Shawn said in awe.

Jared wanted to join in on the excitement, but all he could think about was whatever was behind them, lurking in the darkness. He could feel an invisible set of eyes leering at them, waiting for them to make one wrong decision. That thought was all Jared needed to get moving.

The boys walked for a while. Nothing but shoddy boards on each side with gaps big enough to see the earth behind them. It was a wonder nature hadn't taken back this space with its lack of activity. Thankfully, they didn't come across any other surprises the deeper they went into the tunnel. When Jared thought it was just going to continue going on forever with no answers, the light shone on something up ahead on the left wall.

"A door!" he yelled.

They broke into a run, their feet echoing off the compact dirt with each step. Jared stopped when he reached the door, which was made of solid metal that appeared to be at least a foot thick and had a wheel for a handle.

"Looks like a bomb shelter or something," Shawn said.

"Maybe the door was reused. There's no way they'd build a bomb shelter this far below ground and this deep. It's like a whole damn road down here."

Jared grabbed the wheel and heaved.

It didn't move.

Then Shawn joined him. A grinding shriek echoed through the tunnel. The door shuddered, dust raining from the rusted hinges.

And then—

It gave.

The door lurched open.

Jared stepped inside and lifted the flashlight, revealing rows of dust-covered desks and stacks of aging records.

And across the room was a chalkboard smeared with notes.

Jared's stomach turned cold.

This wasn't just an old shelter.

This was an office.

Jared pulled the door shut so nothing could get in behind them. Then he moved toward the wall, feeling around for a light switch. It was a long shot, but he had to try. He found it next to the door and flipped it on. To his surprise, a single bulb flickered above and remained on. It was dim, but it might as well have been the sun shining in their face after being in the dark for so long. Jared instinctively shaded his eyes, then took in the room. His jaw dropped.

"Holy shit."

"This feels big, doesn't it?" Shawn asked.

"Yeah . . . What the hell is this place?" Jared asked,

walking up to the first desk and checking the drawers. There were countless folders inside. Jared flipped through them. Most were meaningless, until a label caught his eye.

MAIL DAY INITIATIVE.

His hands went numb. His legs buckled.

He collapsed into the chair.

The words on the page blurred as his brain caught up.

He had found it.

The answers.

Part Eleven
The Witching Hour

"What's it say?" Shawn leaned in, his breath warm on his friend's neck.

Jared recoiled. "Jesus, man, did you eat out of Al's dumpster for lunch?"

"Sorry," Shawn shot back. "Forgot to brush my teeth while *saving your life.*"

"Yeah, yeah. Take a seat. Just, like, over there." Jared flipped through the folder, frowning. "It's . . . complicated. Just a bunch of code and nerd shit. We need more."

He couldn't help but feel a bit disappointed that the document he currently held appeared useless to them. He handed the folder to Shawn and scanned the drawers for something helpful. Shawn scrunched his brow as he read the paper.

"Hey . . . what if that thing comes back for us? I know it went the other direction, but we kinda just moved on like it was nothing. Think we need to be worried?" Shawn asked.

"Well, yeah. We have no idea who or what it was. But as long as we're in this room, I think we are safe. The door looks indestructible. Plus, we locked it."

"Yeah. Still, who knows how long it's been down here. Maybe it's hungry. Maybe it likes the taste of human flesh."

"I have the whole town shooting at me. I've seen a giant smoke monster and some tall, creepy asshole sniffing the air for us. Oh, and I killed a man. I'm not as worried about what's out there as much as I would be on a normal day. Plus, one bite out of you and it would become a vegetarian, so I'm safe," Jared said.

Shawn shook his head and chuckled.

Jared got up and moved over to the next desk, intending to check the drawers. Before he decided to open one, he pressed the power button on the old desktop computer below the desk, assuming it was years past operating capability, just sitting here because nobody ever came to clean up the mess. The room looked as if whoever worked down here left in a hurry and never came back. To Jared's surprise, the machine powered on, and an electric thrumming vibrated from inside the computer.

"Wow. This thing still actually works? Let's see what's on it," Jared said.

Shawn rolled over, bumping against his friend's chair. Jared powered up the monitor, which flickered on and off a few times before finally lighting up and remaining on. A loading screen appeared, and the time bar moved slowly, displaying a small loading percentage beneath the graphic.

"Only 4%. This is going to take forever. Let's look through more of these files while we wait," Shawn said.

"Before we do that, there's something I need to talk to you about." Jared wasn't ready to have this discussion, but he wanted to make sure it happened before things got crazy again.

"Talk about what?" Shawn asked, his tone changing from enthusiastic to concerned.

"I know you heard about that figure forming out of the smoke from the factory and that I was there when it happened. But . . . there was a group of people looking for me after Mr. Kaine killed some of the hunters, and the smoke-thing got a few of them. I saw the first person it killed. I didn't wait around to see the second . . . but I *heard* it."

"Damn, sorry you had to see that. What did it look like?" Shawn asked, his curiosity winning out over concern.

"It was scary as hell. Had to be at least twenty feet tall with claws bigger than our entire bodies and a mouth full of razor-sharp teeth. I thought it was just a storm coming, then it started to form like you see in those tornado videos on YouTube. Next thing I know, it swooped in and cut a lady in half with one swipe."

Shawn's eyes went wide.

"That's not why I'm telling you about this now, though. I'm telling you because one of the hunters with the group was your dad. They were all, like, praying to this thing . . . and the mayor told it to take any of the others as a sacrifice if it needed to, but not him. I ran before another person was killed, but like I said, I *heard* it. And I don't know who it was the second time."

Shawn stared at the floor with glossy eyes.

"Dad . . . do you think it got him?" Shawn asked.

"I don't know. Part of me wanted to circle back to see, but I couldn't. I had to get out of there while they were all distracted, you know? Anyways, I just felt you should know. There were a ton of hunters around, so it could have been anyone. But that was a reminder of why we have to be careful with breaking the rules."

"I was supposed to be with my dad, but Wes Tremblay went to Mayor Thompson and demanded I go with him. Said he could use me to find you. I-I was supposed to be there when that happened," Shawn said, the tears pooling up now pouring out.

"Hey . . . we don't know if he was hurt. I just felt like you should find out from me. I know how close you guys are."

"Yeah, well, he's gonna kill me if he finds out I broke the rules to help you, ya know. He loves you, but not enough to put our entire family at risk."

"I really am grateful you're here. I know we made a pact, but in the moment, it's different than playing make-believe out in the woods."

"Would you do the same for me?" Shawn asked.

Jared looked his best friend in the eyes. "I wouldn't think twice. Fuck the rest of the town."

The boys did their secret handshake, a sideways high-five where they gripped one another's hand and pulled in close for a hug, then slapped each other's back three times. Regardless of how this day turned out, Jared knew they would die for each other if it came down to it.

The computer beeped, snapping them out of their embrace. Jared turned and looked at the monitor, which lit up with a strange logo in the center.

"Whoa. You ever seen this design before? Looks similar to what we saw in the dead zones," he said.

Shawn reached out and grabbed the mouse, clicking on the logo. A window opened, taking its time loading whatever it was about to display. The inside of the computer sounded like a factory with all the machines running at once. Jared worried the thing would explode in their faces instead of providing them with any sort of helpful information.

When the blank screen finally loaded, a set of files appeared. Jared's heart went into overdrive. He didn't know where to begin, and while he tried to force himself to read each file name, he found his eyes flitting wildly from one to the next, trying to read them all at the same time. There was so much to absorb, so he forced himself to start at the beginning.

File://recipients
File://immunity
File://deadzones
File://maps
File://skins
File://crisismode

"Holy shit! Which one should we start with?" Jared asked.

"Let's check *recipients*. I wonder if it lists everyone from the past and future," Shawn said.

Jared hesitantly clicked on it, hoping that wasn't the case. This was supposed to be random. If they already had future recipients selected, he couldn't refrain from warning those people. If he even made it out of this alive, that is. The folder opened to reveal hyperlinks to each year dating back to 1890, but it ended with 1985. Jared was mostly relieved that it stopped there, but he was also a bit disappointed.

"That must be the year they closed up shop down here— 1985. These computers sure look that old. I still can't believe they weren't locked by some secure password," Jared said.

"Well, in their defense, it wasn't like this place was located in the back of Al's Diner. They probably didn't see a need to have one with it being like a hundred feet underground."

"If these years are accurate, then all but two of these people died on Mail Day," Jared said.

"Let's check some of them out, see if we recognize anyone," Shawn suggested.

Jared clicked on a random one from 1978, and a picture and bio of a lady named Thelma Lutton appeared. While neither of the boys recognized her, it was still fascinating to read through who she was and how she'd met her demise. Whoever tracked Mail Day down here treated it almost like some sporting event, with a record book, statistics, and locations. They clicked on a few more, but when Jared selected 1910, his blood ran cold.

"Holy shit," Shawn whispered.

It was the Tall Man from upstairs who was talking to Mayor Thompson. Jared knew he looked familiar, and now it was clear why. Reginald Baker was one of the recipients whose family was killed after trying to help him escape. Jared had seen his face in the presentation the mayor gave each year to remind residents why they needed to follow the rules.

"I knew he looked familiar, man. But . . . he died over a hundred years ago. So why the hell did we see him upstairs threatening Thompson?" Jared asked.

"Dude . . . this is weirder than we even thought. What the hell?"

"I don't know. Something about his eyes . . . He definitely didn't look normal. But let's say he was still alive—which mathematically doesn't make any sense—why have we never seen him around town? Where has he been this whole time?" Jared asked.

"Thompson didn't seem shocked to see him. That's what

my mind keeps going back to. You don't think our parents know about him, do you?" Shawn asked.

"No way. They wouldn't hide that from us. We need to focus on why he's here. Let's see what some of these other folders have in them."

Jared minimized the file with Reginald and debated which hyperlink to click next. He decided to skip over the *deadzones* and *immunity* files for now and landed on *skins*.

"Do we really wanna know?" Shawn asked.

"No, but it might have answers," Jared said, then opened the file.

At first, he thought it was just written in some computer code as it appeared to be a bunch of strange symbols and letters running together in one long sentence with no spaces. There were random letters mixed in, but most of the text was written in symbols Jared had never seen before.

"Seems pointless. Let's check the next folder," Shawn said.

"Hold on a sec. If we just pass over it, we could miss something that would help us. Let's at least see what's on these."

Jared selected the first link and immediately regretted it.

An image of a dead body appeared onscreen. Not just any dead body, but a man with his throat slit, his dead eyes staring toward the camera taking the photo. *Staring* right through Jared.

"I think I'm gonna be sick," he said.

"Why would they keep pictures of dead people on here? Sick fucks," Shawn said.

The image was grainy, but that didn't stop it from sharing all the disgusting details. The man was balding, with a black, bushy beard that had blood mixed within the hair, presumably from his slit throat. Jared had seen enough and closed the image. He hovered the mouse over the next link and prepared to open it, but Shawn grabbed his shoulder.

"What the hell are you doing? We don't need to see any more of that, dude. What good is looking at dead people going to do us?"

"It's here for a reason, Shawn. Believe me, I don't want to look at them either, but after killing a man today, seeing a picture of a corpse doesn't exactly carry the same weight anymore. We came down here to get answers. Nobody said it would be easy. You don't have to look if you don't want to, but I *need* to."

Shawn shook his head and muttered something under his breath as the next link was opened. The image that appeared sent a chill down Jared's spine. It was the body of Reginald, his shirt ripped open to display a stomach that looked as if a bomb had gone off inside. His innards were hanging out of the wound—if you could call it a *wound*, it was more like a crater full of gore and viscera. Reginald's eyes were also open, but unlike when they watched him walk by the closet, these eyes were not black.

"Okay. That's about enough of that. This proves he was dead, and *very* dead at that. So what the hell did we just see upstairs?" Shawn asked, backing away from the monitor.

Jared's stomach twisted.

The dates matched.

Reginald was dead.

Had been dead for over a century.

Yet he had stood right there in the hallway . . . breathing, sneering, *speaking*.

Jared's fingers hovered over the keyboard. His mouth went dry.

Then it clicked.

File name: *skins*.

"Oh my god. They're using the dead bodies . . ."

"Using them? What—"

SCREEEEEEEEEEEEEEEEEECH!

An alarm erupted, stabbing into Jared's skull like a buzz saw. He clamped his hands over his ears. It didn't help. The sound was *wrong*—not just loud, but warped, like metal shrieking against metal. Jared squeezed his eyes shut, his vision pulsing.

The Witching Hour had begun.

"What is that?" Shawn yelled.

"I don't know!"

Jared couldn't concentrate as the noise drilled into his ears, scrambling his thoughts. They had to leave, but he still had so many questions. So much to go through. They didn't get any answers on how to end Mail Day. Instead, now they just had more questions than before. Shawn pulled at his friend's sleeve to try and get him to the door. If they stayed in the room much longer, there was a good chance they'd go deaf. But Jared had to keep going. He had to force himself through the blasting siren. Shawn yelled something, but Jared's ears were ringing, he couldn't hear a word his friend was saying. Not that he would have listened anyway. He clicked on the *crisismode* link.

Unlike the other files, this one held only one document.

CRISIS MODE PROTOCOL.

Jared clicked.

The screen flickered. The hard drive whined.

A list of directives filled the screen.

Jared forced himself to concentrate, wishing he had brought a camera or something to take a screenshot so they could get the hell out of the room.

"What's it say?" Shawn yelled.

"Let me concentrate for a minute!"

"What? We need to get the fuck out of here!"

Jared ignored Shawn and read the following:

CRISIS MODE PROTOCOL:

Issued to:

Tunnel Operations Team

Clearance Level: RED

Date: [REDACTED]

NOTICE: This is an active crisis response directive. All personnel must adhere to the following steps without deviation. Failure to comply will result in termination.

1. Immediate Evacuation of Office & Transition to Factory Sub-levels

The office site is compromised. Unexplained power fluctuations and security failures indicate increasing instability.

Remaining personnel must proceed to the tunnels beneath the factory. All monitoring and data collection will continue from that location.

Reason for Relocation: Reports indicate abnormal movements within the office sector. Visual disturbances and auditory anomalies have been recorded.

Last recorded transmission from the office detailed non-authorized entities within the perimeter.

2. Mail Day Protocol: Purpose & Continuation

The event is critical for ongoing research and must be maintained at all costs.

Observational data from the selected recipient's responses is necessary for *Their* analysis.

The compliance of the town ensures that the parameters remain stable. Non-compliance risks direct intervention.

Previous deviations (see [Incident File 1964]) resulted in widespread losses and a permanent removal order.

3. Status of the Subjects ("Skins")

The Skins remain functional but have shown increasing degradation over extended use.

The most recent cycle demonstrated errors in behavioral synchronization. Some have failed to maintain seamless integration.

If exposed to extreme conditions (heat, impact trauma, prolonged separation from the hive), instability increases.

Reports indicate underground movements beyond assigned limits. This suggests some subjects are operating independently.

Further testing required. Any personnel encountering malfunctioning subjects are to report immediately but do not engage.

4. Factory Sub-levels & Hive Management

The Hive remains stable but requires continuous oversight.

The smoke emissions from the factory must be maintained for concealment. Unscheduled disruptions will be flagged as a containment breach.

Last recorded analysis indicated increased activity within the lower chambers. Hive development continues at an accelerated rate.

Personnel assigned to monitoring must avoid direct visual contact beyond Level 3.

Hive integrity is mission-critical. Any damage to the core structure will result in catastrophic failure.

5. Contingency & Final Directives

If relocation fails, activation of emergency protocols is authorized.

All non-essential personnel are advised to evacuate before full hive exposure.

Under no circumstances is unauthorized disclosure permitted. Any breach of information will be subject to immediate correction.

FINAL WARNING

"The balance is fragile. We exist because They allow it. Stay within parameters, and the cycle continues. Disrupt it, and we are expendable."

END OF TRANSMISSION.

"Jared, come on! We need to leave now!" Shawn yelled, snapping Jared's attention from the document.

Testing? Whoever *They* are had been observing Pembroke all these years to see how everyone survived. Jared tried to focus on one thing at a time in the document, but all of it felt important. Most of all, he knew where the team who used to be down here went.

The factory.

It made sense. The smoke-thing came from the factory. He wasn't sure what the mention of a Hive referred to, but he knew the factory was the key.

Jared's pulse pounded. His brain raced to put the pieces together.

The tunnels. The factory. The Hive.

It was all connected.

"The factory," he whispered. "That's where it all is."

Shawn stared at him. "Jared—"

"We have to go." Jared grabbed his bag. His hands were shaking. "We can end this."

Suddenly, the alarm stopped, returning the office to silence. Jared's ears rang, a constant numbing sensation traveling through his head. He realized what the alarm was for.

"The alarm . . . it's for the Witching Hour. We've only heard it a few times and never down here where it's way louder."

"What?! I can't hear a damn thing you're saying!" Shawn snapped.

In truth, Jared couldn't either. He hoped eventually their hearing would return to normal. It was bad enough traveling underground in the dark, adding limited to no hearing made it a recipe for sure death.

"We need to get to the factory," Jared repeated.

Before Shawn could respond, the power went out, sending the office into darkness.

"Shit!" Jared yelled.

"Grab the flashlight. This place is creeping me out now, dude," Shawn said.

Jared felt around in the blank space ahead of him, eventually reaching his bag. He pulled out the light and turned it on. The beam flickered as though it was fighting for its life, then stabilized, providing a cone of illumination.

"Let's get out of here. We have no idea where the factory

is from here, but at least we kinda have an idea of which direction to head," Jared said.

"Do we? I have no fucking clue where we are in reference to the town. It all looks the same down here."

"Think about it. We were in the basement of the town hall, and when we reached the tunnel, we turned left. The factory should be farther down in this direction. Let's go!"

"Fine. But if we get lost down here forever, you won't have to worry about someone from town killing you because I'll do it myself. What did that document say?"

"I'll tell you on the walk. I think we can really do this, man."

They both worked at the iron door together, finally getting it open. Just seeing the emptiness of the tunnel reinvigorated the dread Jared had been able to put aside for a few hours. But it would all be worth it if this plan worked. And for the first time, Jared really believed it could be done. Still, he couldn't stop thinking about some of the buzzwords from the *crisismode* document. *Skins. Hive.* Most of all, two particular sentences kept replaying in Jared's mind.

Reports indicate underground movements beyond assigned limits. This suggests some subjects are operating independently.

Whatever Reginald was, it wasn't really him. It was his "*Skin.*" Something was using it to communicate. And that something was down here. With them.

PART TWELVE
ARE YOU AFRAID OF THE DARK?

After spending hours in the well-lit office, the tunnel felt even darker than before. Jared's ears still rang, and he could only see a few feet ahead of him, even with the flashlight. A crack in the bulb weakened the beam, its brightness lessening by the minute. He prayed it would last until they reached the factory but every few seconds, it flickered as if it was fighting for its last breath.

"I swear to god, if that damn light dies in this tunnel . . ." Shawn muttered.

"We need to pick up the pace. The farther we get from the office, the harder it will be to find our way back if it happens. That was a pretty big drop. I'm shocked the flashlight didn't break as soon as it hit."

"How do you think they built these tunnels? They go on for miles. How did they even get equipment down here?" Shawn asked.

"I have no clue. Look at how perfect the wall and ceiling

curve. It couldn't have been done by hand. The boards on the walls look flimsy, like they were added as an afterthought for support."

Jared continued to rotate the beam of light between the floor and ceiling, making sure there weren't any hidden surprises above or below them. They had been walking for the better part of an hour with nothing but more tunnel in front of them. More darkness. More echoes of every little sound amplified. There were no more doors or ladders to climb up, and the deeper they went, the more he began to wonder if they were heading in the right direction. But then he remembered what skittered in the dark in the other direction when they came down the ladder and what the *crisismode* file had said.

Reports indicate underground movements beyond assigned limits. This suggests some subjects are operating independently.

He had no idea what it meant, but one thing he did know was that whatever crew was down here working, they left in a hurry. And he could only assume that Reginald was one of the "subjects"—the "*Skins.*" What did they mean by "operating independently"? The Reginald-thing sure seemed to be doing what it wanted, not under control by any higher authority. And the mayor responded to Reginald as though he *was* the higher authority. The report indicated there was more than just one of them, and a lot of them at that. It also sounded like they had ambushed the tunnels and forced the research team elsewhere. But something else didn't make any sense, and he couldn't come up with any logical answers.

"Why was the power left on down here? If they've been gone since the Eighties, why not just shut the electricity off so that even if someone did find it, they wouldn't be able to get into the system?" Jared asked.

"Well, like we said earlier, maybe they just knew it would be damn near impossible for anyone to discover it and had bigger issues on their hands to worry about. Like dead people chasing them away. Or . . . or maybe they wanted someone to find it. Maybe they wanted to give someone the chance to end it once and for all," Shawn said.

"I guess. Once we get to the factory, *if* we get there, we have to be prepared for anything, man. Those things could be there. Or the research team that left this office could be there. We don't know whether they would help us or not. I don't see why they would since they'd spent years down here just researching it all without doing anything about it. We also don't know what it is we're looking for once we get there. I just hope it's obvious, you know?"

"Nothing about this is obvious. It's a puzzle that's lasted for over a century. If smarter people haven't solved it, what chance do we have?" Shawn asked.

"Well, it doesn't take much to be smarter than you," Jared said with a grin that was wasted in the darkness.

"Fuck off."

They continued in silence for a few minutes, and all that did was make Jared want to keep talking. The silence brought uncertainty. The unknown. Strange sounds off in the distance that could be something as small as a rat or as big as a human. A *dead* human that somehow moved as if they lived on in eternity. He preferred it when they were talking so he didn't have those thoughts roaming around in his head.

The silence also made him think about his parents, something he hadn't done much since leaving them this morning. *What were they doing right now? Were they hunting for me?*

Like, really hunting me? Or just taking their time, hoping we won't cross paths? They didn't know about Shawn and Jared brainstorming ways to end Mail Day since they were young boys. They didn't know about the Dude Cave or the countless hours spent reading about the town's history. Jared knew that if he had ever informed them of his obsession, they would shoot it down instantly, telling him it was too dangerous to even talk about it, let alone try to do something about it. He wondered if they would even listen to him if he discovered a solution. Or if the town would hear him out. They were all too scared about the possibility of trying to make a stand and get their town back. And Mayor Thompson seemed to have a big investment in making sure Mail Day didn't go away.

That meant it was on Jared. Ending this nightmare, once and for all, would be up to him. He had nothing to lose at this point because he was dead if he didn't survive Mail Day.

"Witching Hour is live, which means they'll have the dogs out hunting. And there won't be an inch of this town that isn't under surveillance. As much as this tunnel sucks, it's far safer than trying to sneak around above ground," Jared said.

"Well, this place gives me the damn creeps, so it better be worth it," Shawn said.

The flashlight flickered, then died, smothering them in darkness.

"Oh, *come* on!" Shawn snapped.

Jared smacked the flashlight, angling it forward. Nothing happened. If they had to trek the rest of the way with zero visibility, he wasn't sure they could make it. If there was no light shining in from whatever exit existed, there was a chance they would walk right past it and miss the factory. *Please work.* He slapped the head of the flashlight again, and it wavered back to life. But as the light came on, something moved up ahead in the dull illumination.

A hunched figure loomed in front of them, its eyes burning through the dark.

"Shit!" Jared snapped.

"What the fuck is that?" Shawn asked.

The figure remained stock-still, facing them with a dead-locked stare. Jared couldn't tell what it was, but it blocked their path.

"What the hell is that?" Shawn whispered again.

Jared didn't answer. Instead, he continued to stand completely still, as if not moving would hide them from the thing. The light wasn't bright enough to see what was behind the figure. Hell, it barely lit the outline of this hunched monster. Was it a person? Those eyes sure didn't look human, but the shape did. He thought back to Reginald and how strange his eyes looked when he walked by the closet. The eyeballs themselves were mostly black with tiny red pupils in the center. Was that what he was looking at right now?

He tried to steady his breath, but it wasn't his breathing he heard. It wasn't Shawn's either.

There was something behind them.

Warm breath tickled Jared's neck. Then Shawn screamed. He whirled around, aiming the light, and came face-to-face with a girl. Her cheeks were sunken in, her teeth rotten to a dark brown. Her eyes matched Reginald's, but the red pupils were much bigger in the dark. Her thin blonde hair clung to her face, but her bangs moved just enough for a crimson hole to appear on her temple. A bullet hole, and from the looks of it, one that was shot at close range. That's when Jared realized who he was looking at.

"Maxine."

"No fucking way," Shawn said, his voice raspy as it recovered from the scream seconds earlier.

Maxine tilted her head, her eerie gaze shifting between them. Every time she breathed out, a rancid odor blew in Jared's face. Her ripped clothes hung loosely, her pale skin almost luminous. Jared wasn't sure what to do; they were now blocked at both ends. But then Maxine opened her mouth wide and screamed in their faces, a deafening noise that echoed through the tunnel.

The boys turned and ran, and Jared noticed that the first figure they saw was no longer in front of them.

Thank God for small favors.

The light rose and fell like a boat on choppy water with each thumping step forward. They kept running, not daring to glance over their shoulders to see if Maxine was following. The beam of light dimmed slightly, shrinking the cone to only a few feet ahead of them. The space was so dark, the shadows swallowing up everything around them.

"Keep going! But watch your step!" Jared yelled, risking a glance back. He wished he hadn't. It was a scene straight out of a nightmare.

Maxine dropped to all fours, scuttling forward. Her eyes blazed in the light. Maxine's limbs bent at odd angles, her elbows and knees snapping upward as she leapt five or six feet with every movement. She scaled the wall, fingers digging deep, then scampered onto the ceiling.

How the hell is she clinging up there like a damn spider?

Jared was so focused on Maxine that he wasn't paying attention to where he was going. His foot hit a pothole, and then he felt himself stumbling forward, close to falling. Shawn caught his arm and Jared regained his footing, hardly losing any speed.

Jared's lungs burned, and he wasn't sure how much longer he could go before stopping to catch his breath. Even with his life on the line, his body could only take so much before it needed to rest. Especially after the day he already had leading up to this. His limbs were rubber. He forced himself to keep moving until Shawn grabbed hold of his arm again.

"St . . . stop," Shawn said through labored breaths. "She's gone."

Jared looked behind him, hesitantly raising the flashlight, first at the ceiling, then to the ground. The space behind them was empty. He closed his eyes as relief flooded him. They had no idea where she went, but for now, she was gone. The look in those eyes . . . While he had seen it on Reginald for a brief second, it hadn't been this close-up, and it wasn't with him screaming inches from his face. Nor had he crawled like some spider-cheetah hybrid with rabies. Maxine *appeared* human on the surface, but whatever that was, it wasn't human.

"That report made it sound like those things were down here doing whatever they wanted. We know there are at least two of them now. But man, I don't know if I can outrun one of them again. My legs are throbbing. My throat feels like something's clawing it from the inside," Jared said.

"Yeah, I'd be good if we never saw that again. By the way, I just want to point out that I saved you. Again," Shawn said.

"Thanks, dude. Let's keep moving. And maybe we should be quiet so we can listen for them. As much as I don't want to hear every little sound, Maxine snuck right up on us while we were talking," Jared said, getting the chills just thinking of her crawling toward them slowly.

"Agreed. How much longer can this damn thing be anyway? We've been going for at least a few miles, don't you think?"

"Yeah, but everything looks the same down here and we were moving pretty slow, so who knows? Plus, the factory is halfway across town from the town hall. Hopefully this is a direct shot and not taking a long way."

As they walked, Jared pulled the backpack off and grabbed two bottles of water, handing one to Shawn. His supply was low, but there was no way they could keep going if they didn't hydrate after all the running. Jared chugged half the bottle, wishing the water was ice-cold but not complaining, then put the cap back on and tossed it in his bag. They moved on through the darkness with the light diminishing every few minutes. Jared's chest tightened at the thought of being stuck in this tunnel with zero visibility knowing those things were crawling around. He shook the thought away for what felt like the hundredth time. It would do no good to scare himself down here. There was enough to do that for him.

What, are you afraid of the dark?

Hell yes, I am. And that's without a bunch of dead people chasing me.

When they reached the area where they saw the hunched figure standing earlier, the tunnel opened up. Like a fork in the road, they had two directions to choose from.

"Shit. Any guesses as to which way we should head?" Jared asked.

"Pull out the map."

Jared did and aimed the light at it, quickly locating the town hall. He traced his finger along the map toward the factory.

"It's hard to tell. Because the factory is pretty much straight across town, so I don't know why we'd have to go either direction from here. Maybe they both meet farther down again before we get to the town hall."

"Lovely. No matter which way we choose, I'm sure it'll be the wrong way. What was our rule out in the woods? Always go left? That way we wouldn't have to remember which direction we came from later."

"Okay. Left it is. Cross your fingers it's not a dead end," Jared said.

"Who cares about a dead-end tunnel? I'm more worried about a dead Maxine."

"Touché."

They veered left, and Jared felt it somehow became even darker than the main tunnel. Every few seconds, the silence was broken up by the sound of something dripping in the distance.

"Maybe that's a good sign? Water coming from an opening above?" Shawn asked.

Jared wanted to believe it too. Even if it was just wishful thinking. Nothing seemed to be going their way down here. Every few minutes, he glanced back, expecting to see Maxine's rotten grin in the dark. The lack of anything pursuing them somehow didn't make him feel any better. Was Maxine just herding them in this direction, forcing them closer to some trap the *Skins* had waiting?

The dripping got louder as they continued moving, but there was still no sign of what was causing it. And then a scent unlike anything Jared had ever smelled came rolling through the path ahead. A mix of vinegar and rot hit him, turning his stomach.

"What the hell is that smell?" he asked, covering his nose with his shirt.

"Disgusting is what it is. It's gotta be whatever's dripping," Shawn said.

As the smell intensified, Jared noticed something. Just to be sure, he turned off the flashlight.

"Hey! What are you doing? Turn that shit back on!" Shawn exclaimed.

"Look . . ."

Jared pointed in front of them, where there was a faint glow fifty feet ahead.

"It has to be the exit. Let's go!" Shawn said, picking up his pace.

"No, hold on. That smell, it isn't normal. Whatever's creating it seems to be coming from up there. We need to be careful," Jared said.

"Think it's something from the factory leaking down below the ground?"

"I don't know. We've passed the factory plenty of times on our bikes and I never smelled anything this nasty. I suppose it could be something that's underground and doesn't waft up above. I still think Maxine was making sure we went this way. She was too fast to not catch up. We should be dead."

"Don't say that. I can't imagine anything worse than her in front of us."

The glow increasingly became brighter, and the smell increasingly matched it. Eventually they got close enough for Jared to realize they had another decision to make. The space in front of them ended, presenting a dirt wall, but they had the choice of going left or right. The light was coming from the left side, and the right side was completely dark like the rest of the tunnel.

"When in doubt, go left," Jared said.

They approached the light, which led to a steep declining

ramp that brought them to another room. Jared couldn't believe what he was looking at. On each side, the wall was lined with glass tanks full of glowing green liquid. It wasn't the tanks that sent a chill down Jared's spine, but what was *inside* them.

Bodies. Suspended in glowing liquid, as if drowned and preserved. They were all about five feet off the ground, and Jared couldn't help but feel like the bodies were staring down at them. But their eyes were closed, their limbs unmoving.

"Okay . . . this is fucked," Shawn whispered.

"Do you recognize any of them?" Jared asked.

Shawn shook his head, but Jared wasn't paying attention to him. He was too focused on the figure floating in front of him, a bald man in his sixties with a thick beard that swayed around in the fluid. He had seen this man before.

"It's Walter Graham. He ran the bar in town until he was the recipient of the envelope when we were little kids. These are all of the skins they keep."

Shawn didn't respond, prompting Jared to turn and find his best friend on the other side bringing his face a few inches from a tank. The row he stared at was much lower, almost eye level with him. A boy about their age appeared to be in a deep sleep. Shawn tapped on the glass like a kid at a pet store.

The boy's eyes opened.

Shawn stumbled back and yelled out in panic, "What the fuck!"

The eyes staring back were black, like those of Maxine and Reginald. The boy's lips curled into a grotesque grin before his mouth yawned open.

Something was floating around inside the cavity of his throat.

Jared wanted to run.

He told his body to do so, but he couldn't move. And then the boy went stiff, his limbs sticking straight out like he was being electrocuted, and his body slowly rotated in the fluid to reveal his back. His wet shirt clung to his bony spine but beneath it, something was moving, pressing against the skin like a baby shifting inside a pregnant mother.

"Jared, we need to go. Now!"

The shirt tore open, revealing taut skin clinging to the bones, and there was a long gash traveling from the lower back and ending between the boy's shoulder blades. Something reached out of the laceration—a long, gray hand. Claws extended enough to be mistaken for steak knives. The inhuman limb pressed against the glass, then slid down the inside like nails on a chalkboard.

Shawn got to his feet and pulled his friend, but Jared couldn't take his eyes off the kid.

"Come on! It's going to break through the glass!"

Jared snapped out of it, then looked at the other tanks and noticed some of them were awakening just like the boy. The odor they smelled as they approached the room intensified and at first, Jared didn't know why. But then he heard the *crack* of glass behind him, and he turned to see the fluid pumping out onto the floor from one of the far tanks. Two arms pried through the back of the skin, clawing at the glass in an attempt to break free.

The boys bolted, plunging into the tunnel's darkness. Jared prayed this was the direction of the factory, and if he was honest, he had lost track of where they went. *Two left turns . . . right? Just remember that.* As the green glow faded to nothing, glass shattered behind them.

"They're out! Go!" Jared yelled.

He grabbed the flashlight, attempting to turn it back on

while running. The light flickered but came to life. Jared aimed it behind them and shone it at two crouched figures scurrying into the tunnel. There would be more to follow.

As he turned to point the light in front of them, it grazed Shawn's shoulder, falling from Jared's grasp. It was as though everything next happened in slow motion. Jared stopped, trying to catch the flashlight before it fell. It flipped through the air, briefly pointing at the ceiling before the beam whirled back around, highlighting the hunched figures running on all fours. And then it smashed off the floor, sending the tunnel into complete darkness.

"No . . . no, no, no," Jared whispered.

"We have to take our chances in the dark, man. Come on!" Shawn snapped.

They picked up the pace, unable to see even a few inches in front of them. It was a strange sensation, like some void had swallowed them up and they were running through an infinite dark loop. Jared lifted one hand as he ran, blindly feeling the empty space in front of him.

They couldn't see the *Skins* behind them, but they could hear them.

Breathing.

Growling.

Moving on hands and feet like a pack of demon-possessed monsters.

Jared couldn't get the image out of his head of something digging out of the kid's back, its clawed fingers prying apart the pale skin as a set of hazy eyes stared out. *What are these things? And how are they part of Mail Day?*

His thoughts were interrupted by a bellowing cry from behind them.

"What the fuck was that?" Shawn yelled.

"Keep . . . going," Jared panted.

Every step felt like it would be the wrong one, that they would land in a divot and roll an ankle. As much as Jared wanted to run full speed, his brain wouldn't allow it, hesitant to give maximum effort when there was no telling what surrounded him.

"Whatever that scream was, I think they stopped following. I need a break," Shawn said.

Jared didn't want to stop, but Shawn was right. They were no longer being pursued.

"None of this makes any damn sense," Jared rasped. He was really struggling to speak; his throat felt like it had been scraped with sandpaper. "I know what we just saw, even though I wish it wasn't real. But why are they down here? What's the point of keeping past recipients in tanks?"

"I stopped trying to figure out what the hell was going on when I saw something clawing out of that kid like it was a costume."

They moved faster, trying to put as much distance between them and the *Skins* as possible. The idea of being hunted at full speed was terrifying. But being stalked? That was worse.

The *Skins* were taking their time. Which meant they didn't think Jared and Shawn could escape.

"Seriously, though. Who was writing down all those notes we found? Was it the people in charge? Or people like us trying to find answers?" Jared asked.

"No idea."

Jared reached out to the side, sliding his hand along the wall. The cold, rough surface grounded him. At least they weren't moving through a void. But the familiar suddenly felt foreign. Was that rough wood? A spiderweb? A cobweb? If it was a web, were there mutated spiders waiting for a warm body to stumble into their trap?

"All I know is I can't wait to be out of this damn tun—"

Jared's foot caught on something. He tripped and slammed face-first onto the dirt.

"You okay?" Shawn asked.

"There's something here. Hold on . . ."

Jared felt around blindly, fingers trailing over fabric, and then, a rip in the cloth. Beneath it, something leathery and hard. A warning bell went off in his brain, and he jerked his hand away, shaking it like he could rid himself of the contamination.

It was a corpse.

Jared jumped to his feet as a chill went up his entire body.

"What is it?" Shawn asked.

"S-someone died down here. It's a body, and I just touched it. I fucking *touched* it. I think I'm going to be sick."

Jared swallowed hard, forcing the nausea down. It wasn't just the fact that there was a body. It was the *why*. Why was someone lying dead in the middle of the tunnel?

"Maybe it's the rumored escapee they never found?" Shawn suggested.

"I don't know. But we need to be careful. What if worse things are lying in wait down here? I'm glad those things stopped chasing us, but it doesn't make any sense why they gave up."

The discovery rattled Jared more than he thought possible. The tunnel felt wider, yet he felt trapped. A strange, suffocating sensation of mental claustrophobia.

They kept walking in silence, every step measured. The strange, vinegar-like odor from the tanks finally began to fade. Jared doubted he'd ever be able to eat fish and chips again. It was a random thought, one that had no place in this moment, but it still made him sad.

The boys crept forward. One step. Then another.

The darkness was absolute. A black so deep no eye could pierce it.

No human eye, at least. But those things sure didn't have any trouble.

Jared tried to steady his breathing, unsure if the tightness in his chest was panic or something worse. He couldn't stop thinking about the corpse. Was it an old *Skin*, discarded like a used tissue?

The wall was cold and jagged. Jared kept his hand against it as they pressed deeper into the tunnel. A seemingly giant, carnivorous maw swallowing them whole.

"This has to end soon," Shawn whispered. "I don't know how much more I can take."

"You and me both," Jared muttered. "I feel like I keep hearing those things creeping behind us. Every sound makes me want to piss myself."

"Nothing new there. Didn't you wet the bed until you were, like, ten?"

"Real funny, asshole."

Jared slid his hand along the wall until suddenly, it wasn't there. He froze.

"Why'd you stop?" Shawn asked.

"The wall ends. We've reached another intersection. There's a path to the left over here. Go check the other side."

"Hell no! You want me to walk across the tunnel?"

"Want me to hold your hand?"

"Screw you, man. If I trip over another dead body . . ."

Shawn shuffled away. After a minute, his voice called out,

"It's all solid over here. If we go left again, we might just loop back. I say we keep going straight."

A scratching sound moved along the ceiling.

Jared's stomach dropped.

Please, no. Not Them.

Jared turned back. Shawn must have done the same. Two tiny red dots blinked on the ceiling.

Then more.

And more.

They were everywhere.

"S-Shawn . . . run!"

The silence shattered. A mass of bellowing screeches erupted from the darkness.

The *Skins* had been toying with them. Stalking them. *Herding* them.

Jared ran, hoping Shawn was beside him, hoping they were heading toward the light. They had to be close.

"Up ahead! There's a glow! I think we're there!" Shawn shouted.

Jared pushed himself faster, heart hammering. Twenty feet ahead, the tunnel opened into a wide space. A faint glow seeped in—not green like the tanks, but natural light.

Jared risked a glance back.

Some of the *Skins* were still wearing their human bodies. But two of them had shed their disguises, revealing gray, sinewy creatures with large black eyes and beady red pupils glowing like embers.

Jared's stomach twisted into knots. He had only seen their limbs before. Now he saw them whole.

No noses. Just long, black slits where nostrils should be. Mouths full of fangs sharp enough to carve through bone. Their ashen skin glistened, covered in thick slime.

The vinegar scent hit him like a punch.

Jared didn't look back again.

Up ahead, a rope ladder dangled from the ceiling. It was their way out.

If they could make it in time.

As the *Skins* closed in, Jared reached the ladder, with Shawn right behind him.

He grabbed hold of a rung and started to climb, feeling a sudden sense of vertigo as the ladder swayed in the open space.

Sweat sheened his face, the fear of heights kicking in more with each step.

Still, that fear took a back seat to the things chasing them. Shawn grabbed a rung below him and started to climb, which caused the ladder to sway back and forth even more. Jared clung to it, and all he could think was, *After all this, this is the way I'll die.*

"Hurry, Jared! They're coming!" Shawn yelled.

"I'm fucking trying! The ladder keeps moving. I can see the top! We're like halfway."

As he said it, he looked down and felt sick to his stomach. The ground was dark, but he could still see that a fall from this height would kill them. The creatures that shed their skins climbed up the side of the rock wall while those still wearing them attempted to go up the rungs behind the boys.

Jared shifted his focus back to the door above and picked up speed.

His hands were clammy, but he squeezed tightly, making sure that if he fell, it wouldn't be because of something as ridiculous as his hand slipping.

With the door now close, he could see that it resembled something you would see in a bunker, with a thick metal wheel similar to the office door they entered earlier and a dome-like arch. The light leaking in came from cracks between the door and the wall.

Finally, Jared reached the door, clinging to the last rung with one arm as he reached up to try and turn the wheel above. Shawn caught up to him, panting uncontrollably.

"Hurry! They're right below me!"

Jared risked another look down and saw two of the human Skins only ten feet below them, climbing quickly. The creatures on the wall were already level with them, but the walls were far enough from the rope ladder that they couldn't reach without jumping from the wall.

They wouldn't do that, would they? Risk their own lives to get us?

The boys were surrounded on all sides except from above. Jared put as much force behind his push as possible, feeling the wheel move a few inches as it groaned from years of being locked in place. The creatures on the wall hissed, reaching out with their claws. Even though Jared knew they were too far away to reach him, he couldn't help but feel they were going to latch on and tear his body to pieces.

He pushed again, and the wheel spun, making a loud *click* indicating a latch disengaged.

As he went to push up on the domed door, A scream tore from Shawn's throat, raw and desperate.

Jared glanced down and saw that one of the *Skins* had reached him, grabbed hold of his foot, and was pulling downward. Shawn kicked at the thing with his other foot, but then both his feet slipped from the rung, leaving him hanging by his hands.

"Help! Get it off me!"

Jared's heart pumped in his ears, drowning out the screeching from the wall creatures.

His best friend was about to die if he didn't do something.

He quickly slid the backpack off while holding onto the rung with his free hand. He realized the *Skin* grabbing Shawn was Maxine. The bullet hole in her temple leaked a green substance as she snarled.

Jared waited for a clear shot, then threw the backpack down, watching as it smacked her face.

She lost her grip and went flailing through the air, knocking another one of the *Skins* off the ladder as she dropped in a free fall. The *CRUNCH* of her body hitting the ground echoed up through the tight space.

Shawn placed his feet back on the rungs and waited for Jared, who returned his attention to the wheel. He pushed up with all his strength, shocked at the weight of the door, and light blasted in from above.

The creatures on the wall bellowed in agony when the brightness hit them.

The sound was deafening, and Jared's instinct was to cover his ears, but he knew that if he did, he would drop from the ladder and meet the same end as Maxine.

He climbed through the opening, then turned and reached to help his best friend up. When Shawn climbed out of the door, he dropped to the floor panting, and Jared glanced down into the tunnel a final time, seeing one of the creatures on the wall smoking. Its red pupils expanded, and then it lost its grip on the stone, shrieking as it fell from the wall.

Jared slammed the metal door closed, locating a locking mechanism and latching it shut.

The sounds from beneath were drowned out for the most

part, but he could still hear the muffled screams from the remaining creature and *Skins.*

One of *Them* pounded on the inside of the dome, but it wasn't budging. Confident that they couldn't break through, Jared turned back to Shawn, who was now standing and staring at their new space.

"I think this is the basement to the factory, man. We made it," Shawn said.

Jared dropped, letting his body relax for the first time in several hours. He wanted to cry, but he was too exhausted. They made it. They were one step closer to ending Mail Day.

"The sun . . . It hurts the ones not wearing skins. That's why they use them. It's almost dark outside, and there's only a little light coming through the basement window, but that was enough to hurt them."

"Then why the hell did those few get rid of their humans? Why put themselves in danger?"

"Well, they probably didn't think we would blast them with light. But I think it was more than that. There were two of them out of their skins. There are two of us. I think they wanted our bodies," Jared said.

He closed his eyes and took a deep breath. This was all so much bigger than anything he could have ever expected. But they were close, he could feel it. Now they just had to figure out what to do at the factory to end this nightmare forever.

Part Thirteen
Don't Play With Fire

Jared sank onto the cold floor.

He shouldn't have.

His muscles were lead. His head swam. Every breath felt like it had to claw its way up his throat. His limbs weren't just weak, they barely felt like they belonged to him anymore.

And now he didn't even have water to replenish his energy because he'd thrown the backpack at the Maxine *Skin* trying to pull Shawn off the ladder.

"Hey, I saved *your* ass this time. We're even," Jared said.

"You have some ground to make up, but I'm not picky. Thanks for that. Dude, my fingers were so damn close to slipping when she was pulling on my foot. I really thought I was a goner."

"Here's my thinking," Jared started. "The *Skins* use the human bodies to hide themselves to walk among us undetected and as protection. They obviously aren't human. I don't know if they're aliens, demons, or something else. Whatever the hell they are, the light burned the one that didn't have a human skin on. Not that we will know who's a *Skin* and who isn't, but at least we know a weakness.

"Also, that explains why they keep them down there—to stay out of the light. I'm not sure if the tanks were to let them adjust to their new bodies or what. Whatever that liquid was creating that nasty-ass smell, it wasn't water."

"So, the file you read said the researchers had moved here —to the factory—but maybe there isn't anything in the basement that will help us," Shawn said.

"I don't know. The ladder from the tunnel brought us to the basement of the factory. I don't think they'd have anything on the ground level where everyone could see it. There must be something down *here* that we have to find. Something that controls their whole operation."

They sat in silence for a few minutes, and Jared had never wanted a drink of water so badly in his life. Maybe they could find a sink in the factory. Hell, he'd drink from a toilet bowl right now. They didn't just lose their water, though . . . they lost food, their light, and the map.

"Damn it. The map was in the bag, man. I know there's a dead zone around here, but I don't know if it was *in* here or not. Maybe we should try and keep the talking to a minimum, at least. Search this level, then work our way up if we have to," Jared said.

He didn't want to move, but he knew they had to get searching. He wasn't sure why, but it felt like they had to do something before the end of Mail Day in order to end it. That if they waited until the morning, it would be an entire year before they could try again. Sure, he'd survive the night and have immunity, but what about Shawn? What about his family? He wanted to protect all of them, not just himself. There was also the issue that kept creeping back in his thoughts—Shawn helped him. Even if Jared survived, would the town do something to Shawn and his family once they discovered he was aiding Jared?

"Shit, remember the Witching Hour is live. Things are going to be extra hard up on the surface," Shawn said.

"Wish I still had the bear spray with me. At least that would throw off the dogs."

"That's what I smelled at the Dude Cave! Glad I stole it from my dad's stash. Guess in a way, I saved your life again," Shawn said with a smirk.

"I'll be sure to remember that next time a *Skin* is trying to pull you to your death."

"Too soon, man, too soon."

They got up, and Jared fought off the throbbing pain in his quads and hamstrings, determined to find the answer they sought. While it wasn't the visceral darkness of the tunnels, the basement to the factory wasn't very well lit either. Jared was just thankful he could at least see a few feet in front of him. This room didn't appear to be important, so they moved through it, glancing at shelves that were mostly empty. There was a constant buzzing noise pulsing from somewhere, and Jared assumed it was the generator or whatever powered the factory.

"Do you even know what this factory produces? I can't believe I've lived here my entire life, researched the town, and still have no idea," Jared said.

"It's some type of metalworks foundry my dad said. I didn't care enough to keep asking. But now that you mention it, it does seem odd that nobody ever talks about it. It kinda just sits in the background of town doing its thing and everyone ignores it. Do you know anyone who even works here?"

"I think I remember my mom saying a few of her friends did. Didn't mention who. That's about it. I just assumed every town had its own factory."

A junk pile of old equipment sat in the corner of the room, but just like the room itself, it appeared useless. Jared spotted another door behind the equipment and headed for it. He hadn't necessarily expected immediate answers when he reached the top of the ladder, but to say this room was a disappointment was an understatement. Still, the adrenaline resurfaced as he searched for any meaningful information. Nobody had ever attempted to end Mail Day, too selfish to protect themselves from death. Had Ms. Hendrix explored this same area? Did she have the chance to save the town and had chosen to save herself instead? Jared couldn't bring himself to be that selfish. To turn a blind eye on everyone you spent your entire life growing up around just for the chance to escape while everyone else lived on in fear . . . Somehow that felt as bad as killing the recipient of the envelope.

Jared opened the door in the corner and was hit with the scent of gasoline emitting from within the dark space. It was strong enough to burn his nostrils, but he'd take that smell over the pungent odor in the tunnels any day. The new room didn't have as much light as the last, but it still offered more visibility than running through the black hole below. The smell wasn't the only thing in the space. There was a humming noise coming from somewhere. Jared couldn't put a finger on what the sound was, but it was a distant vibration, and even though it didn't sound close, it started to scramble the inside of his head.

"What the fuck is that?" Shawn asked, holding his hands over his ears.

The sound vanished.

Jared swayed.

Something was wrong—*more* than wrong. He tried to recall the last few minutes, but his mind was full of static, like a corrupted file. A blank space where his memory should be.

A shiver rolled through him.

Had it just stolen time from them?

"Dude . . . did you piss yourself?" Shawn asked.

Jared looked down at his pants and even in the dark, he saw the giant wet spot on his crotch. Shame and embarrassment overtook him until he noticed Shawn had done the same thing. His best friend noticed him staring and looked down at his own pants.

"Well, fuck me."

"Whatever that sound was, it did something to our bodies. I don't know how much of that we could take before it kills us," Jared said.

"What happened? I remember walking from the tunnel door and checking out the other room, and that's it."

"I-I don't know, man."

Whatever had happened, it gave Jared a splitting headache. His sinuses didn't react well to it either. He wiped his nose as it began to run, snot trickling down. When he pulled his hand away, a streak of red smeared across the top of his fingers. Before he could panic, he saw Shawn's nose doing the same thing. It was as if something had shot through their entire body, throwing off all the normal senses like a bunch of faulty wires. They had to leave fast.

"Let's get the hell out of here," Shawn said as he wiped the blood on his shirt.

They moved on to the next room, and the source of the gasoline smell revealed itself. An oversized generator sat in the corner, chugging along. Multiple cans of gas were lined neatly next to it.

"Is this what made our entire body vibrate?" Jared asked.

"Maybe. The fact that there's gas down here and an operating generator tells us people from town know about this area. I think that must mean some of the residents are involved with the mayor."

"How could a secret that big stay hidden, though? This place isn't exactly buried in the woods. It's a giant metal foundry sticking out like a sore thumb."

"I don't know. But we need to be careful. People were here recently enough to put gas in this generator," Shawn said. "Who knows how often they have to do it?"

"Which brings up another question. Where did the people from the office below go? The new office has to be in here somewhere," Jared said.

"Their research area could have been down one of the paths we didn't choose in the tunnels. There's a whole lot of space we didn't explore," Shawn said.

They passed the generator, and Jared was just happy the vibrating sensation didn't return. The inside of his head still felt rattled. If he had the time to be concerned with something powerful enough to give them bloody noses and make them piss themselves, he'd be freaking the hell out right now. But it wasn't at the top of the list of terrifying things witnessed in the last hour, let alone their lives.

As they moved to the next room, more strange machinery lined the walls. Jared had no idea what the inside of a metalworks foundry even looked like, so this could be completely normal, but his gut told him the equipment they were looking at had nothing to do with the factory. It was like one giant engine down here, powering some unknown world. Heat radiated off the equipment on each side, and Jared was grateful when they reached the end of the hall and turned left into another room. Shawn held up his arm, stopping Jared from advancing.

"You hear that?"

"Dude, my ears are still ringing from that vibration. How the hell are yours working fine?"

"Quiet. I'm serious. It's coming from up ahead somewhere. Like a squirming sound," Shawn said.

"Lovely. Be prepared for anything," Jared whispered.

They crouched and moved quietly through the room and rounded a corner. Jared had warned Shawn to be prepared for anything, yet what sat in front of them was something nobody could prepare for. The room was dark (still providing more light than the tunnels did), and it was difficult to know for sure what they were looking at, but this could be sitting in the sun as clear as day and it still wouldn't make any sense. The tank loomed in the dark, its glass warped with age.

Inside, something pulsed.

A writhing mass of limbs, spines, and twisting flesh slick with slime. Arms tangled with legs, torsos fused together in a grotesque knot of bodies. The creatures weren't separate anymore. They were one.

As they got closer, Jared realized the limbs weren't human; they were those of whatever the hell the creatures were that wore the skins. A sharp icicle of fear stabbed his chest. The things appeared to be sleeping, molded together in a giant ball of squirming parts.

"I think it's their nest," Jared whispered.

"Holy shit. We need to get rid of it. Think about it, man.

Whatever the hell these things are, they're linked to Mail Day. If we can destroy *Them . . .*"

"We end Mail Day," Jared said.

It was too dark to see their features clearly, but it appeared as if their heads were all buried in the center of the mass, their arms and legs wrapping around one another as though they were huddled together for warmth.

I'd like to provide some warmth. Light the fuckers on fire.

"The gas! We can blow this factory to the damn moon. Melt these freaks," Jared said.

"*Shhh.* If you wake them, I don't want to be around for it. And how exactly do you plan to start a fire? We don't have a lighter or matches."

Jared thought for a second. He remembered when he and Shawn had gone through Cub Scouts together, one of the skills their scoutmaster taught them was how to start a fire with two twigs if you were stranded in the woods. It had been a few years, but if they found something that could create a spark, Jared felt confident they could do it.

"We need to look for anything that could make a spark. There's gotta be something here."

"Hell yeah. Let's split up, but be careful. We stay in the same room, just spread out. Got it?" Shawn asked.

"Sounds good."

With that, the boys dispersed, searching the dim corridor for anything that could ignite. There was no telling if this would work, even if they *did* get the place lit up like the Fourth of July. And then there was the question of how dangerous it would be to breathe everything in when the smoke spread around town. Still, Jared knew in his heart this was the way to end it. The factory was their base. Their home. Their *nest.*

As a little kid, Jared's parents had always told him how dangerous it was to play with fire. Now, that skill might actually save his life and the entire town along with it. The old metalworks factory had to have something that would spark. The boys searched for close to twenty minutes before Jared spotted a rusted toolbox near a set of lockers.

He scanned the contents, praying there would be a box of matches or a lighter. With no such luck, he lifted the top tray and rummaged through the bottom storage area. He was just about to give up and move on when he spotted a round file meant for sharpening the teeth of a chain saw.

This will work!

Jared moved aside a few wrenches that were too smooth to create friction, then found one that was beaten-up from years of use. He quickly rubbed them together, feeling the two surfaces resisting against one another. A small spark flickered and with it, Jared's heart rate intensified.

"Dude, I got it!"

Shawn rushed over from the other corner of the dark room. Jared showed him, and the boys high-fived as if they had just done something as simple as beating a video game together. It was a stark reminder that they were just kids. Kids who didn't get the satisfaction of living a normal life like most boys and girls in the world.

"We need to douse the area around the tank in gas and cross our fingers that a small spark can ignite a fire. Then we need to get the hell out of here before it blows," Jared said.

"That's the other problem, man. We don't even know where to go from here. What if we light this place up and then can't find the exit?" Shawn asked.

That was something that hadn't crossed Jared's mind. To

him, it was as simple as climbing up until they found the door. But what if the door was locked from the outside?

"As much as I want to do this, you're right. Let's just double-check to make sure we see a way upstairs first. We also don't even know what time it is. The Witching Hour started a while ago, so my guess is it's at least, like, ten p.m."

"I don't know. There was still light coming in from the windows a little bit ago. I'm not sure that much time has passed," Shawn said.

"I think the vibration made us lose track of time, though. We don't remember anything from right before it. I saw a door past the Hive of freaks out there. Let's check that first," Jared said.

They slowly crept by the mass of entangled limbs, listening to the squishy suction sounds coming from within the tank. Even in the dark, Jared swore he saw some of the faces buried in the center of the nest watching him. It sent a trickle of fear down his spine. The door he mentioned opened with a rusty groan, causing him to wince. He didn't dare open it all the way, just enough for them to squeeze through. The boys had already been chased by some of these things earlier, no need to set off round two.

After they both made it to the next room, Jared took a deep breath.

"What do you think the difference is between the tanks we saw earlier with one body in them versus whatever the hell that was out there?" he asked, pointing toward the previous room.

"If I had to guess? The single tank is where each creature adjusts to their new body, and the nest is where they all come together for power, or food, or something."

"So fucking creepy. I still can't shake the feeling that this place could be hidden for decades from the rest of town yet be right in plain sight. I get the tunnels. They would be impossible for most people to discover. But this? And what the hell are all those *Skins* even here for? Why are *They* forcing Pembroke to play this fucked-up game every year while hibernating beneath the ground?"

"I don't know if we'll ever get answers to most of that. As long as we end it all, do you really care? Sure, I want to know more. And we'll probably wonder for the rest of our lives. But if we are the ones to end this, and we make it out alive . . . I won't lose another minute's sleep trying to solve this damn puzzle," Shawn said.

Jared thought about it as they walked, coming to a stairwell. Shawn was right. At the end of the day, what mattered more than anything was finding out how to end it, not what caused it or what motivated *Them*.

The stairs were made of metal, their feet clanking on each as they ascended to the next floor. When another door presented itself, Jared opened it slowly, happy to discover that this one didn't open with the same rust-induced shriek. He poked his head into the room, scanning the dark space for any sign of people or *Skins*. The room was quiet. Only equipment and stacks of boxes were visible. Then, what he saw in the far corner made him smile.

An *EXIT* sign.

"This is our way out! We're going to do this, man. Let's blow this place."

The boys made it back to the generator room and headed straight for the gas cans. Jared was pleased to discover that they were indeed full of fuel, something they had forgotten to check earlier. They each grabbed a can and walked to the Hive room. Jared couldn't help but feel like an arsonist, that he was doing something extremely illegal and would go to jail for the rest of his life.

Yeah, well, murder is illegal too. That doesn't stop the whole town from trying to kill its residents.

They emptied two entire cans of gasoline around the perimeter of the tank, pausing a few times throughout to make sure the creatures weren't awakening. After everything they had been through, it felt as if this was going too smooth. Jared wasn't about to question it, though.

"Okay. Fingers crossed, this spark will be enough to light the fire."

As Jared grabbed the file and wrench, he only had a second to hear the buzzing sound again before the thrumming shot through his body. This time, it was much louder, and it was clear that the source of the vibration wasn't the generator, but the Hive. He dropped to his knees, holding the side of his head as his vision blurred and shook. He could make out just enough to see the mass of creatures in the tank twitching to the buzz and the fluid bubbling.

Just like before, it was over as quickly as it started. The creatures pulsated in the tank but remained as one. Jared looked at Shawn, who was also on the floor, his nose bloody once again. There was no telling what kind of permanent damage this was causing to their bodies. Jared's head pounded, but he needed to push through it and try to start the fire.

He staggered to his feet and grabbed the tools again.

"You okay, man?" he asked Shawn.

"My head is killing me. But I'll be okay. Let's hurry."

Jared ground the metal together. Nothing.

Again.

Nothing.

Sweat dripped down his temple. The gasoline fumes made his head spin. *If this didn't work . . .*

He struck again.

A spark leapt through the air like a tiny shooting star, landed on the gas-soaked fabric—

And ignited.

But the spark died before it reached the ground. Suddenly, the gasoline fumes were making him lightheaded, and he needed to take a break.

"There's too much distance between the spark and the gas," Shawn said.

"Do you suggest I put my face down there and set it on fire with the factory?"

"No. But I have an idea."

Shawn ripped some of his shirtsleeve off, then kneeled and soaked it in the gas puddle at their feet.

"I never thought I'd say this, but you're a genius," Jared said.

"Thanks, I know. That's the second time you've said that today. Here . . . I'll set it on the edge of the tank. Try to get the spark to land on the cloth."

After trying for a few more minutes, Jared felt like he was watching it in slow motion. The spark flying from the metal-on-metal friction. Sailing through the air. And then finally, the bright orange trail landing on the gas-soaked sleeve. The cloth ignited instantly, but Jared had to get it in the puddle below. He carefully reached out with the wrench and poked it off the edge of the tank, sending it onto the gas-soaked floor.

A cloud of flames shot high, almost lighting up Jared, but he jumped back just in time to avoid it. The hair on his forearm had been singed, leaving a painful blister. The fire quickly spread around the base of the tank and wouldn't take long to spread to the generator and the rest of the metalworks factory.

"We need to get out of here!" Shawn yelled.

Jared clutched his burned forearm and nodded, but he wasn't ready to leave just yet.

"We need to make sure this works."

"Need to '*make sure*'? Are you fucking high? The place is going to blow!"

The flames climbed the walls, latching on to anything consumable. Shawn pulled at Jared's arm, which finally snapped him from his trance as they moved toward the door to the stairwell. Shawn reached the steps first. Jared stopped and took one last glance back at the nest. The flames worked their way up around the structure, but the tank still held firm. And then the meaty mass of *Skins* began to move. Untangling from one another, screeching so loud it could be heard through the fluid, through the glass, over the roaring fire.

Multiple sets of red pupils stared at him through the smoke, claws pounding at the tank. Shawn again pulled on Jared, but not before he spotted what his best friend was watching.

"Holy shit."

The fire exploded outward, a shock wave of heat rolling over Jared's face.

The *Skins* screeched.

The tank cracked.

Jared grabbed the door handle, his hands slick with sweat. The fire hadn't reached them yet, but it would. He slammed the door shut, twisted the dead bolt.

And behind it, the glass shattered.

At the very least, he knew it would slow *Them* down,

hopefully long enough to cook their bodies until they were charred black and peeling apart.

As the boys made it up the stairs and into the next room, something exploded below, shaking the foundation of the factory.

"We need to get out before the generator catches!" Shawn yelled.

They headed for the *EXIT* sign, and Jared couldn't help but wonder where the hell all the researchers were located. Were they in here being burned alive with the *Skins?* There had been no sign of them. It was too late for that now anyway. Jared and Shawn reached the door and burst through it, out into the night. They kept running until they reached the tree line a few hundred feet away. Once they thought the distance was safe, they dropped down, catching their breath, panting in both fear and exhaustion.

"What now?" Shawn asked.

Jared thought about it for a moment and only one answer came to him.

"We wait."

Part Fourteen
It All Comes Crashing Down

Smoke poured into the night sky, thick and black, clawing upward like a living thing. Even from here, Jared could feel the heat—waves of it rolling off the burning factory. It would only be a matter of time before the flames spread with it. The fire was hungry. If the explosion didn't happen soon . . . the town would put it out. And everything they did would be for nothing.

"We have to stay hidden until it blows. If they find us first, we might not get the chance to prove our plan worked," Jared said.

Shawn nodded, and they continued waiting. Panicked shouting closed in, coming from multiple directions. Then flashlight beams bounced off the surrounding trees. Dogs barked. The Witching Hour was in full effect, and the boys had just put targets on their backs.

"The factory, it's on fire! We need to put it out immediately!" Mayor Thompson yelled from the road. "Someone get Cheevers down here now! Tell him to bring the fire truck."

Jared risked lifting his head above his cover to determine how many people were coming. He felt sick to his stomach. A group of at least ten to fifteen residents followed the mayor, and they all carried weapons. Jared crouched back down and turned to Shawn.

"There's a lot of them. I'm not sure this place will explode before they can put the fire out."

"What do you think we should do?" Shawn asked.

Jared considered their options. If the mayor was not the one leading the pack, he might risk jumping up to warn the hunters. Not only did Thompson want Mail Day to remain intact, he would also demand that someone kill Jared and Shawn on the spot for conspiring against the rules and putting Pembroke at risk.

"I still think the best bet is to wait this out. We should be far enough away from the building to avoid any debris from an explosion."

"What about the dogs? They'll just set them loose on us and say *screw it* if someone gets immunity. This is bigger than anything that's been tried before. Plus, we've heard the stories about what happens to people who break the rules," Shawn said.

"It's too late for that, man. We've seen what's down in those tunnels. We know more about Mail Day than anyone in town outside of Thompson and maybe Ms. Hendrix. This place needs to burn to the ground before we can show our faces again."

Residents yelled and screamed at one another, running around in a state of panic. The fire had spread to the main level of the building, and the smoke continued to seep out of cracks in the windows, polluting the air. It brought Jared's thoughts back to the smoke monster that had come from this very building and killed two residents. Could it happen again? This time to him and Shawn?

Jared crawled to the base of a large maple tree to get a better view. Shawn lifted his arms as if to ask, "What the fuck are you doing?"

He needed to know who was with the mayor. The last time he saw his parents was at the town common first thing this morning, and as ridiculous as it seemed, just the sight of them would make him feel better right now. He had been too busy fighting for his life to think much about it, but with everything he had been through today, everything he had seen —the death, the destruction, the monsters—he had the sudden urge to find his mom and dad. Jared envisioned running up to them and giving them a bear hug, squeezing and never letting go. Hell, he would even tell them he loved them, which was a big no-no for a teenage boy expected to resent his parents.

The mayor stood front and center, directing residents who were happy to help. Shawn's dad was with a few of his work buddies, and while Jared couldn't hear what they were saying, Mr. Spears was pointing to the surrounding woods on the other side of the factory. One of the other guys nodded and headed for the forest. It would only be a matter of time before others searched the side where Jared and Shawn hid.

Behind Shawn's dad, Jared spotted Al from the diner and a few teachers he recognized from his school. Even with the dark night sky and a forest full of trees to hide them, he couldn't help but feel as if multiple sets of eyes were watching his every move. With his attention focused on the crowd of people, which grew by the minute, he didn't hear his friend sneaking over to him.

"Are you trying to get us killed?" Shawn whispered.

"I'm just scoping the scene. Your dad's over there. He sent one of his friends out in the woods looking for me. Do you think he already knows you're with me?"

"No way. I'm sure they're wondering where I am, but they don't think I'd fuck up this bad. Even if we make it out of here alive, I'll be grounded for life."

An explosion from the factory blew out one of the windows, sending glass spraying in every direction. Someone screamed. Mayor Thompson snapped at another resident, asking where the fire truck was. The force of the blast blew a powerful gust of wind through Jared and Shawn and down toward Main Street. It wasn't until one of the dogs started growling that Jared realized the breeze had revealed their scent.

Harper, the German shepherd that belonged to Jared's English teacher, Mr. Roberts, bared his fangs, barking aggressively toward the trees.

"Shut that mutt up! We need to get water, now!" the mayor yelled.

"He doesn't do this for nothing, Thompson. He smells the boy. He's close," Mr. Roberts said.

Jared felt a lump rise in his throat.

"So let the dog go sniff him out then!"

"I'm not letting Harper near that building alone. Not until the fire's out. Let me go search for Jared with my dog."

"Fine. Whatever. Just let me think a minute to figure this out. Do what you gotta do."

Mr. Roberts grabbed the dog by the collar and whispered something in its ear, then he released the collar, and Harper took off ahead of him toward the woods. Toward Jared and Shawn.

"Shit . . . I need to say something, Shawn. Stay down and let me talk."

"What? Are you stupid? They'll shoot you on the spot!"

"We'll both die if I just hide and wait for them to find me. I need to do this."

Before Shawn could object, Jared stood from his hiding spot and walked out of the forest with his hands held high as if surrendering would stop them. There was no waving the white flag in this scenario. There was survive or die.

"He's over here!" Mr. Roberts shouted.

The crowd of residents murmured, talking amongst one another, then followed Mr. Roberts and Harper. The dog was getting dangerously close.

"Please! You want immunity? You want to survive? If you kill me, only one of you gets it. But if you listen to me, we all do. Just . . . give me one chance. That's all I ask," Jared said, trying to sound confident. But on the inside, his heart pounded violently and his nerves twisted around his muscles, begging him to sit down before they gave out.

"He's just trying to save himself!" someone yelled from the swarm of people.

"Yeah, he's put us all in danger! Kill him!" another shouted.

Jared's biggest fear was becoming a reality. They were too scared to listen. He had disturbed the order. He needed to get their attention.

"The factory is their home. *They* live underground, controlling the town. Mayor Thompson knows this! When the factory blows, so will their nest. And with it, the rules of

Mail Day will end forever! Please, just give me a chance to prove it!"

Mr. Roberts turned to face the mayor with a look of agitation and confusion, snapping his fingers at Harper to stop the dog from proceeding.

"This true, Thompson? You knew of a way we could end this shit, and you kept silent?"

The mayor scanned the crowd, likely trying to find some of his strongest supporters. Or maybe even some of his co-conspirators. *He can't be the only one who knows about this.*

"The boy's just trying to save himself! Making stuff up so we won't try to kill him! We all know what happens when we don't follow the rules!"

More back-and-forth arguments escalated in the crowd.

"All I ask is that you wait and see what happens. If I'm wrong, well, you won't have to go far to find me. I'm right here and I'm not going anywhere."

He saw some of the adults conversing, looking at one another in confusion. There were at least *some* of them who wanted to believe. But for every resident who appeared willing to hear him out, there were just as many—if not more—who wanted to kill him, like they would a rabid dog that threatened them.

"You got five minutes to explain yourself, kid," Mr. Roberts said. He held his dog by the collar, preventing him from attacking.

Harper made it difficult to focus on talking, but Jared knew he had one shot to get it right.

"There's a tunnel . . . It starts under the town hall and goes all the way to the factory. It's intentionally hidden, and Thompson knows about it. He hid it from us. For some reason, he wants Mail Day to stay in place. *They* give him something in return. He—"

"That's enough of this! I'm not about to listen to some stupid kid, the recipient of the envelope for that matter, try to slander my name to save his own ass!" Thompson yelled.

"Quiet, Thompson. We'll hear what he has to say, then make a decision on what to do," Mr. Roberts said.

"This is bullshit! *I'm* in charge here, not some third-rate English teacher. Someone . . . get the kid now!"

Jared watched in disbelief as many of the residents pushed and shoved, some trying to get to him while others attempted to hold them back. There were punches thrown, and just when he didn't think it could get any worse—

A single gunshot.

He covered his face, expecting to feel the painful burn of a bullet lodging into his chest or stomach, only nothing happened. Nothing except for the crowd going silent, as if the bullet killed their rage.

He opened his eyes, double-checking his body for a wound which hadn't triggered the part of his brain that registered pain. When he realized he wasn't hurt, Jared lifted his gaze to the crowd, which had now parted like the Red Sea.

Sam Cronin emerged, holding the gun out as if it was contagious. One look in his eyes broke Jared's heart. He realized his dad would do what had to be done. It was going to be Maxine Kaine all over again.

"Dad . . ."

"Son, why? Why would you show yourself right now? You were so close to beating this. It's only a few hours until daylight, don't you get that?"

His dad's words came out defeated. Even with the night sky, Jared saw his glossy eyes, tears slipping down his cheeks.

"You have to believe me, Dad. We can end this! In the tunnels, there's an office. They did all the research there about Mail Day. There are these . . . *things* that live down there, controlling the whole town. The creatures wear dead people's skin to appear like us, but they're monsters, Dad. Their nest is down there, and I think they're living off our fear, or . . . something. I don't know exactly why they're doing what they're doing, but if we get rid of *Them*, Mail Day is over. That's why I lit the factory on fire."

He paused, waiting to see if his dad or anyone else reacted. The mayor scoffed, but he didn't dare speak with Mr. Roberts standing close by.

"How do you know the building blowing up will end things?"

"I-I don't know for sure. But it's their nest. If we destroy it, *They* can't control us."

"The kid sounds fucking crazy! Monsters wearing human skin? A *nest*? Your boy's read too many comic books, Sam!" Al shouted.

This triggered more complaints and doubts. Jared was losing the crowd and with it, his chance of survival.

Another powerful explosion went off in the factory, crumbling part of its structure. Debris flew in every direction, smoke and fire creating a ball of flames that shot up like a nuclear blast. Jared fell to the side, again wondering if the contents in the factory—and what lay *beneath* it—could blow the town to smithereens, rendering all of this useless.

Red lights flashed off the trees surrounding the factory, and Jared realized it was the lone fire truck in town making its way down Main Street toward the factory. The siren drowned out all the residents and Jared's attempt to beg for his life. Some of the crowd turned to look, distracted by the sudden blare. Jared's dad didn't budge. Instead, he stared at his son, the gun trembling in his hand.

Is he really considering shooting me? Where's Mom?

"Dad . . . please. You have to believe me," Jared said so quietly that he doubted his dad even heard him. His voice cracked, then the dam broke and tears flowed down his face. His dad cried as well. The father and son ignored the rest of the crowd, which turned out to be a big mistake. Someone screamed behind his dad, jarring Jared's attention.

"If you won't do it, I will! Move out of my way, Sam!"

Shawn's father pushed a lady out of the way, forcing her to the ground, then barged past Jared's dad, raising his pistol. While Jared saw compassion and uncertainty in his dad's eyes, Shawn's dad had one intention in his.

"Mr. Spears, please listen to me. It's over!"

"Sorry, kid. I loved you like a son."

Mr. Spears steadied his aim, and all Jared could do was remain frozen in place.

The fire spread up the side of the factory, lighting up the area in an orange hue. As Shawn's dad prepared to fire, a painful shrieking sound came from inside the factory.

The Skins.

Like a horde of wasps trapped in a poisoned nest, they roared in agony, and Jared pictured them trying to break through the basement door to safety. Just when he thought it couldn't get any worse, the buzzing vibration returned, only this time it was far more powerful than when he and Shawn were in the basement near the genera-tor. All the residents dropped to the ground, clutching their ears as they screamed in pain. The dogs, including Harper, yipped and whimpered before tucking their tails and taking off through the woods in an effort to distance themselves. Seemingly, the *Skins'* cries coincided with the vibration.

Al clawed at his face, digging into his eyes as blood poured from his nose and eye sockets. The lady next to him, who Jared assumed was his wife, vomited, then crawled to her husband. The owner of the diner appeared to be having a seizure, experiencing the vibration far worse than others.

"Look what he did to my husband!" the lady cried.

Finally, the buzzing stopped, and the returning sounds of the fire truck overtook the ringing in Jared's ears. His relief was short-lived as he remembered what was about to happen before the distraction. He turned to find Mr. Spears fixated on him, gritting his teeth as he again aimed the gun at his son's best friend. Blood oozed from his nose into his mustache.

"I'm sorry, son."

Jared braced for the bullet.

Then—

Impact.

He hit the ground hard, his head snapping back against the dirt. Pain shot through his ribs. For a split second, he thought he'd been shot.

Then he heard Shawn scream.

Jared's stomach dropped.

He whipped around just in time to see his best friend on the ground, blood soaking through his shirt.

"Shawn!" Jared yelled.

Mr. Spears dropped his gun and ran to his son, his face full of absolute terror.

"What did I do?! Shawn!"

It suddenly clicked. Shawn had pushed Jared out of the way. His dad accidentally shot him. *No, no. Please let him be okay*. It was an image straight out of hell—Mr. Spears on his knees, holding Shawn who was paler than the moon, so much blood saturating his shirt. The factory burning in the background as the shrieks of the *Skins* were muffed by the fire.

Sam Cronin ran to his son's side, and then Jared spotted his mother pushing through the crowd to reach them. She looked awful, exactly like one would expect a mother to look when forced to hunt for her own kid in an attempt to kill him.

"I'm sorry, I was off in another part of town and came as soon as we heard the explosions. Sam . . . what are they going to do with him?"

Jared's dad didn't respond. Instead, he just shook his head and glanced over at Mr. Spears holding Shawn. That bullet was meant for Jared, and his dad knew it.

As everyone adjusted to what just happened, the residents had taken their focus off not only Jared, but the factory. The shrieking had died. Hopefully the *Skins* died with it. The fire had now consumed the entire building, and the handful of volunteer firefighters hadn't yet gone to work trying to put it out. Maybe they never would.

The crowd started arguing again.

"People! We still need to do what's right! The boy needs to die. Before it's too late!" Mayor Thompson insisted.

"We need to give the kid a chance to prove his story!" a man yelled.

"Yeah! Did you really know about the tunnels?"

"It's your fault we're stuck in this?"

The questions and accusations were flying from every direction, and the mayor was losing control of the town. Before he could respond, someone screamed behind him. The crowd turned toward the cries.

A wet, choking sound cut through the arguing crowd.

Jared turned.

A woman was crawling.

Her white hair was stained red. Blood poured from her mouth as she dragged herself forward, gasping.

Behind her, he came.

Reginald.

Towering. Silent. Smiling.

Mayor Thompson dropped to his knees, holding up both hands as if in worship.

"Please. There's still time! It-it's not even daylight yet!"

Everyone watched in shock as Reginald stared down at the old woman who was losing strength by the second, then lifted his foot and stomped down on the back of her head.

The residents gasped. The old lady did not. Her head disintegrated beneath the weight of Reginald's foot, popping like an overfilled balloon. Thompson stopped begging but remained on his knees, waiting for Reginald's next move.

"The boy has ruined our home. He's ruined everything. Someone must suffer for this."

His enlarged black irises burned into the crowd of people. Nobody dared to speak. Finally, the mayor got to his feet. Jared cowered behind his parents as Thompson turned and pointed at him.

"The kid is right there. We can sacrifice him right now in front of you!"

"You are useless to me."

"No . . . I can fix—"

Reginald's hand lashed out, fingers closing around the mayor's throat.

Thompson gasped, clawing at the viselike grip.

"P-please," he choked.

Reginald tilted his head—curious. Then, in one savage motion, he ripped.

Skin, muscle, and bone tore free.

The mayor collapsed, his body twitching in the firelight. His blood pooled at Reginald's feet, steaming in the night air.

Another explosion went off in what was left of the factory. The ball of fire lit up Reginald's hideous features as the structure came crashing down behind him. Reginald stepped over the mayor and locked eyes with Jared.

"Now . . . Now you pay."

PART FIFTEEN
RETURN TO SENDER

Jared remained behind his parents as Reginald stalked toward his family. The red dots in the centers of his eyes pulsated and with it, brought another small vibration in Jared's head. Was Reginald controlling the buzzing the whole time?

"Don't come near our son! It's over," Jared's dad said.

Reginald stopped his pursuit and just stared at the Cronin family, his black and red eyes scanning each of them, *devouring* them. His shirt and suspenders were drenched in the mayor's blood, and some of it had spattered onto his face. The glow of the fire highlighted every detail of his features, revealing a set of jagged teeth fit for a shark.

"I suppose now that the boy knows what we are, there's no need to play dress-up anymore. You all had it so good. All you had to do was follow our rules. Now, this useless scum is trying to end everything we've built on this world. Just know, it didn't have to go this way."

Before anyone responded, Reginald's face began to shift.

The skin rippled as something moved beneath. The red in his eyes brightened, and one look into them made Jared realize he'd made a huge mistake. Yes, the nest was destroyed. But all that did was piss off their leader. Mail Day might be over, but his life was about to be as well.

Reginald's body shuddered, his spine ripping through his flesh like a serrated blade.

His clothes tore open, seams splitting as his bones stretched and rearranged. A wet, tattering sound echoed as jagged ridges punched through his back.

Exposed. Shifting. Alive.

And then a growl. Deep and primal.

Not human.

Jared instinctively backed away, unable to take his eyes off the beast, yet terrified to watch the shift from human form into some monstrosity. Again tearing the flesh of its previous owner, Reginald's legs stretched, growing to lengths taller than Jared's entire body.

Reginald towered over Sam and Mel Cronin, but they didn't budge. Jared wanted to tell them to run. Get as far away from this nightmare as possible. But he also sought their protection, as false as that security might be. He *needed* it. The Reginald-thing lifted its arms, which had also extended to inhuman lengths, and tore at the skin trying to cling to its body. Beneath the pale flesh, the dead gray color of the *Skins* appeared.

"You pathetic little humans . . . I'll kill each and every one of you," Reginald vowed. Then his human face stretched, going taut until it ripped down the center, tearing away like a rotten banana peel. The facial structure Jared had gotten used to seeing in the tunnels revealed itself. Reginald's human skin fell to the ground, and the residents gasped at the horrible sight before them. Someone screamed, others shouted amongst themselves, but none of them came forward to defend Jared or his family.

After everything Jared had been through, all the death and destruction, it was all for naught. His entire family was going to be mutilated and there was nothing he could do about it. Reginald lifted one of his massive, clawed hands, preparing to strike.

"Enough!"

Reginald froze, and the crowd turned to see Ms. Hendrix approaching from the road. The red lights from the fire truck continued to flash as the flames expanded, burning the factory to a pile of rubble.

The Reginald-thing snapped his alien head toward Ms. Hendrix and roared, sending strands of saliva flying through the air. Jared couldn't believe that of all people who might try and help, it was an old lady who didn't need to. She already had immunity. Why would she put her life on the line?

"Draxion, it's over. It's time we leave these people alone. The boy has defeated the pact, and you need to accept that," Ms. Hendrix said.

What the hell? How does she know Reginald? Or . . . Draxion? Jared wanted to know.

The beast snarled.

"*Pact?* No. They give one. We take. We live. They end us, so we end them. Over and over," Draxion said, his speech now more primal with his human disguise gone.

"No! Enough damage has been done. We can find another place. Leave them alone. Do you understand me?"

"Ms. Hendrix? How . . . how do you know this thing?" Mr. Roberts asked from the crowd.

She turned and looked at all of them, taking her attention off Draxion.

"The Ms. Hendrix you knew is long dead. She passed a year ago. But before she did, she found me. Deep in the tunnels. Among the others. And she spared me. I was the only one of our kind to feel any sort of sympathy for your people. She could have killed me, but she didn't. She let me live."

The crowd again argued with one another, trying to figure out what was going on.

"She hid among us! She can't be trusted!" someone yelled from the crowd.

Draxion stepped forward, approaching Ms. Hendrix from behind.

"Watch out!" Jared yelled.

"He won't attack my back. Draxion knows better." She resumed her story. "When Ms. Hendrix showed me compassion, I offered peace to her and a way to escape. At the time she was a young woman and selfish. She saved herself, but she couldn't *live* with herself. Before she died, she came to me in the tunnels, which, for an old lady, is no easy task. Just ask these boys. She asked me to end it. To bring peace between our kind and yours. I told her that I'd help the next recipient. Our kind selects the recipient of the envelope each year, and I knew it would be Jared Cronin because I influenced the decision.

"So, I gave the boy subtle hints. He's a smart young man and picked up on them. I knew what he and his friend were up to the last few years, trying to find ways to save this town instead of just worrying about themselves. I knew he'd be the one to do it. I didn't want our species to die, but there was no choice. There's been enough death, Draxion."

Jared couldn't believe it. Ms. Hendrix wasn't Ms. Hendrix

at all. She was a *Skin*, disguised as a human, trying to help humans. Everything clicked into place: the reason Ms. Hendrix talked to him specifically, the fact that she knew the town hall was a dead zone, and hinting at it being a place to hide. Jared wished Shawn was alert to witness it all.

Shawn . . . Is he going to live? Am I going to live?

"I demand you step down. *Now*. Don't make me do something you'll regret," Ms. Hendrix said.

It was so odd seeing an old, frail-looking lady command such a presence, so confident in her orders to a giant monster. Jared imagined she must be one of their leaders, maybe even their queen, if they had that sort of hierarchy.

Draxion didn't move. His muscles tense, as though he was forcing himself not to attack. He breathed heavily, staring at Ms. Hendrix. His gray body glistened with a thick slime as the towering fire consumed the sky, reaching for the moon. Draxion flexed his claws, his expression unreadable. Residents whispered to one another, too afraid to flee. He stepped over Reginald's torn flesh and kneeled, facing Ms. Hendrix. He stared at the ground, seemingly worshipping her, then raised his face in defeat.

"They were never meant to live."

His mouth lifted in a twisted smile, then he turned and lunged, driving his elongated claws into the face of Jared's dad. Blood sprayed onto Jared as his mother screamed. The tips of the claws broke through the back of his dad's head, and Draxion raised his arm with the claws still firmly lodged in Sam Cronin's skull, lifting the body high above his family.

Jared couldn't move. One minute, his dad was fine and protecting him, and the next, he was viciously attacked before they even had a chance to blink.

Draxion slammed Jared's father onto the dirt.

A sickening *CRACK* split the air.

His spine—shattered.

Jared gaped, but no sound came out.

His father lay there, eyes open, still reaching.

But he was gone.

The monster stared at the limp body, panting wildly, then turned his attention to Jared.

"Don't worry, it's your time to join him."

Jared was so focused on Draxion that he didn't hear the crowd screaming and fleeing, nor Ms. Hendrix shedding her skin. And then he sensed another towering figure in his peripheral vision stepping toward them. He pried his eyes away from his dad's killer and looked over at what used to be Ms. Hendrix, only now she appeared almost identical to Draxion except with a female build.

Without another word, she flew through the air, colliding with the beast, sending them both airborne toward the forest until they slammed into a soaring maple tree. The base of which cracked, sending it crashing to the ground. With the *Skins* momentarily away from them, Jared crawled to his parents.

"Mom . . . is he alive?"

Jared knew it was a dumb question. But his brain was not willing to believe his dad was dead. Not after all they had been through. His mom didn't respond, unable to speak as the sobs took hold. She clutched her husband in her lap, holding his face to her stomach, cradling him like a baby. Jared couldn't see his dad's face, and he knew that was a good thing.

Behind them, Mr. Spears was still tending to his son. It looked like a war zone, with blood and bodies scattered across the ground. The strobe effect of the fire truck lights coupled with the glow of the spreading flames added to the haunting scene. The factory had been forgotten in all the commotion, and the fire was now reaching for the trees.

A loud *CRASH* from the forest startled the remaining crowd, and they watched as both *Skins* ripped and clawed at one another. The one that had worn Ms. Hendrix's skin jumped on Draxion's chest, driving him into a towering oak, which snapped and fell against a smaller tree to create a domino effect. She swiped at his face, knocking him back out to the clearing. His body tumbled and slid across the grass ten feet, bringing him far too close to the Cronin family.

"Mom, we're not safe here!" Jared yelled, trying to get her attention off his dad.

She finally looked up at him, and one look in her eyes broke his heart. He wanted to mourn his dad with her, but they would be dead as well if they didn't move.

Draxion got to his feet, a green fluid dripping from a few fresh wounds. Ms. Hendrix was too strong for him. She attempted to swipe across his face, but he was ready this time. He caught her clawed hand in his grip, squeezing so tight that Jared heard tendons and bones popping and cracking. Ms. Hendrix roared in agony, then Draxion flung her through the air. Her body smashed off the side of the fire truck, creating a massive dent in its side. She fell to the ground, quickly trying to get to her feet. But Draxion wasn't going to let that happen. He leapt through the air, making up the distance in a single jump, landing on top of her back.

He tore at her gray flesh, digging his claws into her rigid spine. Then he grabbed her by the back of the head, driving her face repeatedly onto the ground.

Jared knew if she died, so would the entire town. Draxion would see to that, and he'd make them suffer greatly while doing it. He could hear Ms. Hendrix's face being rearranged every time it connected with the hard earth.

Draxion lifted her head, staring into her glazed eyes.

"You choose them over your own. You die with them."

Ms. Hendrix fought to stay conscious, but it was clear she was close to being knocked out, or worse. Draxion squeezed the back of her head and lifted higher, preparing to deliver the killing blow. But before he could, gunfire rang out. And not just from one gun, from many.

Jared glanced at the pack of Pembroke residents who didn't run to safety. These were the people who wanted to believe Jared ended Mail Day. The people who didn't want to sit back and follow a set of barbaric rules that had been in place for over a century. They aimed and fired, some with handguns, others with shotguns. Bullets tore into Draxion as he jerked back, dropping Ms. Hendrix onto the ground.

The gunfire continued, with numerous stray bullets and shells hitting the fire truck and forest beyond. But many connected with their target, dropping the monster to his knees. Draxion steadied himself, planting his massive claws into the earth, and raised his head. His black and red eyes didn't display pain or fear as one might expect. They radiated anger and rage. He opened his mouth, exposing countless teeth that could rip someone's head off in a single bite. A mixture of thick saliva and alien blood poured forth. He growled from deep within his chest, and Jared knew he was about to pounce.

Draxion coiled, muscles bunching.

Ready to kill.

But Ms. Hendrix pounced. Her claws sank into the sides of his skull, puncturing deep.

Draxion's eyes bulged. His mouth opened, but no sound came.

With a savage *SNAP*, she ripped his head to the side.

His spine tore.

His body collapsed, twitching, oozing.

Ms. Hendrix stood over him, Draxion's head still in her grip.

She looked at the dead face staring back at her. A single tear slipped down her gray face. She stared at the crowd of people, who all continued to aim their weapons at her, unsure if she was a threat. Jared waited for her to say something, *anything*, but she had said enough. She crouched, guns still pointing at her, and launched herself into the forest, clearing a number of trees and disappearing into the night.

Whatever her name really was, she saved the town as well as Jared's life. He would always remember her as Ms. Hendrix. Jared kept his eyes locked on the trees, hoping she would come back so he could thank her. But he knew she wouldn't.

With the *Skins* no longer a threat, people began talking again. Relief and grace replaced the fear and agitation that existed earlier. The remaining residents checked on one another, making sure everyone was okay.

Jared set his hand on his mom's shoulder, feeling her violent sobs shaking her body. He wasn't so sure she saw any of what just happened. Instead, she hadn't left her husband's side. The three of them sat there for what seemed like minutes before Mr. Roberts approached them.

"I'm so sorry. Your husband, your dad, he was a good man. He didn't deserve this. But it's over. Thanks to you, Jared. Thank you."

He didn't know what to say. Part of him was relieved and

happy that Mail Day was over. But the town would never be the same. His dad was dead. His best friend was on the verge of death, the last he knew. So many residents lost their lives tonight.

"You know, he told me earlier today that he'd rather die than see his own son killed. He was willing to blow this whole thing up if it meant saving you, Jared," his mom said.

Jared had been strong for her up until now, forcing the tears down, even though his own dad was gone forever. Hearing her say that ruined any chance he had of remaining strong. He cried, and he cried hard. He buried his face in her shirt, now blood-soaked—his dad's blood—and let her hold him.

When there were no tears left to shed, he again thought of Shawn. He needed to know if his best friend was alive.

I can't lose someone else. Please let him be okay . . .

"I'll be right back, Mom."

She nodded as Mr. Roberts remained at her side, trying to comfort her. Jared headed toward Shawn and saw Mr. Spears still on his knees, leaning over his son. He paused, suddenly too nervous to move, receiving flashes of Mr. Spears trying to shoot him, his eyes crazed as he pulled the trigger. A man he looked up to was willing to kill him without batting an eye.

But his relationship with Shawn won out. He'd face a whole clan of *Skins* if it meant getting to his friend. He stepped up to Mr. Spears, who turned to see who was behind him.

Jared wasn't sure what to expect in his eyes, but it sure as hell wasn't shame. Mr. Spears averted eye contact with him, staring at the ground.

"Jared . . . I'm so sorry, kid. I . . . I—"

"It's okay, Mr. Spears. You were only following the rules.

Trying to protect your own family. I'm not mad at you. Is . . . is Shawn going to live?"

It was hard to get the words out. He couldn't imagine life without his best friend. They did everything together. Jared hesitated to bring himself to move past Mr. Spears. From his current position, all he saw were Shawn's legs.

"He's a stubborn little guy. I think he'll pull through."

"Jared?"

He almost didn't recognize the raspy voice, but it was Shawn. Jared stepped around Mr. Spears and forced himself to look at his best friend. His shirt was covered in blood, and his skin was sweaty and pale. But he was smiling.

"We did it, man. We fucking did it," Shawn said, then remembered his dad was there. "Sorry, Dad. Didn't mean to curse."

"I'll let it slide, since I shot you and all. Probably owe you more than that, huh?"

"Oh, you know it. I'll be expecting pizza every night for the next two weeks," Shawn said with a smirk.

"Done," his dad agreed.

"Wow, that was easy. Three weeks?"

"Don't push it, kid."

"Hey, man, I just wanted to thank you. I'd be dead if it wasn't for you," Jared said.

"Suppose I saved your life again, huh? Guess we're not even after all."

"Guess not. It got my dad. He-he's dead. I don't know what to do. Mom needs me, but all I want to do is cry around her. I can't live without him," Jared said. He felt more tears coming but pushed them off.

"Be there for your mom. The bullet went through my

shoulder. Hurts like hell, but my dad helped to stop the bleeding. I'll be fine. Your mom needs you," Shawn said.

Jared wiped at his eyes, feeling fortunate that he didn't lose his friendship. He held out his hand and kneeled, and without a word, Shawn knew what he wanted. They did their secret handshake, then Jared got up and headed back to his mother, staring at the scar he and Shawn had carved into their palms last summer.

He wasn't sure they would get all the answers to Mail Day. Who were the researchers? Where were they now? Who was working with Mayor Thompson to make sure the secret of the *Skins* and the tunnels remained hidden?

Jared didn't care about any of that right now. Mail Day was *over!* He reached his mother, who was getting help from a few of her friends. She saw him and pulled him into a big hug. In that moment, he thought everything would eventually be okay. But no matter how hard the town tried to forget, Pembroke would always remember.

Acknowledgments

I have many people to thank for this one. First, my Patreon subscribers, because without you, this book wouldn't exist. It was my first attempt at serializing a book, and you all made it worthwhile. I hope the experience was as fun for you to follow along as it was for me to write! Thank you to my wife and kids, for having the patience while I wrote two novels simultaneously. One novel takes up enough time, writing two at the same time took up far more time. Thank you to my editor, Danielle Yeager, who continues to be amazing to work with. She's thorough, efficient, and very collaborative throughout the whole process. If any of you were wondering who did this awesome cover, look no further than Christian Bentulan. I can't thank him enough for the amazing work. Once again, I want to thank Steven Pajak for working his magic with the formatting inside. He's extremely talented, and one of the nicest dudes in the industry. And thank you to all of my readers who continue to support me through every project. It's a dream come true to have a following that looks forward to each release.

A SPECIAL THANK YOU TO MY PATRON MEMBERS

Alicia Toothman
Crystal Evans
Janeth Acevedo
Julia Terry
Leanne Meyer
Liz Wallace
Mary Trujillo
Megan Stevens
Meredith Livingston
Paige French
Sophia McIntyre
Steven Jeczala
Trina Thompson
Aaron Masters

Gage Greenwood
Molly Mix
Nancy Crowley
Stephanie Winegeart
Andrea Wright
April Butler
Jay Bower
Megan Stockton
Tyler Shields
Carisa Kyle
Jim Donohue
Tim F
Shanda Langley
Nicole Sonnenburg

ABOUT THE AUTHOR

John Durgin is a proud active HWA member and award nominated author. Growing up in New Hampshire, he discovered Stephen King much younger than most probably should have, reading *IT* before he reached high school—and knew from that moment on he wanted to write horror. He had his first story accepted in the summer of 2021. His debut novel, *The Cursed Among Us* was released June 3, 2022, and went on to become an Amazon bestseller. Next up, his sophomore novel titled *Inside The Devil's Nest*, released in January of 2023, followed by his debut collection, *Sleeping In The Fire* in June of 2023. In 2024 he released two more novels, starting with *Kosa* which released to stellar reviews, and *Consumed by Evil* through Crystal Lake Publishing in November 2024. His most recent novel is The Devil's In The Next Room.

facebook.com/John_Durgin_Author
x.com/jdurgin1084
instagram.com/durginpencildrawings
tiktok.com/@johndurgin_author

WANT A SIGNED COPY OF JOHN'S BOOKS?

Want a signed copy of John's books? Visit his online shop for swag, signed books, and more!

ONLINE SHOP

OTHER WORKS BY JOHN DURGIN

The Cursed Among Us (Book 1 of the Newport Curse series)

Inside The Devil's Nest

Sleeping in the Fire: A Collection of 9 Horrifying Tales

Blank Space

Kosa

Consumed By Evil (Book 2 of the Newport Curse series)

What Swallows The Light- Suffocating Skies (Dark Tide book 19)

The Devil's In The Next Room

Coming soon from John

Conjuring The Demon (Book 3 of the Newport Curse series)

November 2025

Yule (Mid-grade horror novel)- **December 2025**